Gently in the glens

At first, she was merely a pleasant diversion, an object of amused speculation for Superintendent George Gently and his wife and relatives on a June holiday in delectable Perthshire: a painted lady with her light-of-love.

The next day, the wild and lovely country beneath Ben Lyon had swallowed her up, and an urgent police investigation was afoot to locate her and her fleeing boyfriend, and to placate an enraged husband.

The breakdown of a personality and its awesome consequences is evoked in an exciting story, set in a locale of great beauty by a master of suspense.

Other murder cases investigated
by Chief Superintendent Gently, CID.

GENTLY IN THE GLENS

Alan Hunter

Constable · London

First published in Great Britain 1993
by Constable & Company Limited
3 The Lanchesters
162 Fulham Palace Road, London W6 9ER
Copyright © 1993 by Alan Hunter
The right of Alan Hunter to be
identified as the author of this work
has been asserted by him in accordance
with the Copyright, Designs and Patents Act 1988
ISBN 0 09 472690 6
Set in Linotron Palatino 10pt by
The Electronic Book Factory Limited, Fife
Printed in Great Britain by
Redwood Books, Trowbridge, Wiltshire

A CIP catalogue record for this book
is available from the British Library

In memory of my sister
Ethel Mary Hunter

1

'It makes me sick,' Bridget said. 'Surely she doesn't have to be quite so obvious.'

'Oh, I don't know,' Geoffrey grinned. 'The age of permissiveness, and all that.'

'Would you want her for a client?'

'Ahem! She'd need toning down a bit for a court appearance. But I think she'd be smart enough for that. I've had pros who you could pass off for vicar's daughters.'

'And that simpering kid. He's half her age.'

'Oh come on, Bridgie! She isn't more than forty-five.'

'Fifty if she's a day.'

'Well, he must be nearing thirty.'

'It doesn't matter. I think she's disgusting.'

They were drinking sundowners outside The Clachan, Gently, Gabrielle, and Gently's sister and her husband. The soft boom of the falls was in their ears and the sun had just slipped behind the hill that was facing them. An occasional car crept across the bridge opposite, where visitors still strolled or paused to gaze at the falls. The Clachan, Kinleary, on a soft June evening, with every one of the outside tables occupied.

'I saw them arrive,' Bridget sniffed. 'You lot were inside getting the drinks. He was all over her, rushing to open her door. That red Sierra with the stupid sticker.'

'"I support Rangers",' Geoffrey read, squinting. 'They'll be a couple from Glasgow on the spree. But never mind, Bridgie. We're here, that's the main thing. And I'm going to paint that view across there for a start.'

'Oh, you and your painting!'

7

'Still, we're here. After three torrid days on the road. What do you say, George?'

Gently drank, shook his head. 'I think we're due for an early night,' he said.

'I'm dropping,' Gabrielle said. 'And those beds looked marvellous. Tomorrow we can think what we shall do, yes?'

But still they lingered over their drinks at that perfect place on that perfect evening. And Bridget had the satisfaction of seeing her scarlet woman led into the hotel on the arm of her toy-boy.

It was a friend of Bridget's who had recommended the cottage in that delectable part of Perthshire, and at first Gabrielle had been doubtful about returning to a land that held such poignant memories. But, with a map, Gently had shown her that Perthshire was far removed from Sutherland, and a little reluctantly she had agreed to the projected fortnight at Fern Cottage.

On the Friday, Bridget and Geoffrey had joined them from Somerset and had slept on a shake-down in the lounge at the flat; then on Saturday they had got away early, and escaped the worst of the traffic as they left the capital. Alas, their good fortune was not to last. They struck their first A1 jam at St Neots. The next was just beyond Newark, and the third required a detour through Tadcaster. At Boroughbridge they held a conference and elected to turn off through Wensleydale, but jams hit them again at Penrith, and miles of cones stretched northwards from Carlisle. They conferred again in a steaming lay-by.

'I've had enough,' Bridget said firmly. 'This is our second day on the road, George, and I want a shower and a meal and a bed.'

So they'd checked the map, and chosen Moffat, and booked rooms at The Annandale Arms hotel, and Geoffrey had rung the keyholder of the cottage to let him know that they wouldn't be arriving till the morrow. And after all it made a pleasant break, in that small town surrounded by hills, a gentle foretaste of things to come when the crowded roads were left behind.

But – not yet. The Sabbath or no, they hit cones at Abington

8

and Wishaw, were crawling forever by Cumbernauld and jammed for an hour at Stirling. And there, at last, things did begin to ease, as they turned off to head for Balmagussie, where they arrived at mid-afternoon and parked to search for a late lunch.

'This is where it begins,' Geoffrey said, gesturing to the braes that hemmed the town, to the ben that loomed at the end of the main street. 'Here is where we leave Glasgow behind.'

They had found lunch in a pub, and not only lunch: a tall, gaunt figure was propped at the bar. It turned to reveal a large, mournful face, and grey eyes that suddenly opened wide.

'Good grief, man – it isna – it cannot be! But is it yourself, after all this time?' And in a moment he was pumping Gently's hand, and reaching for those of the others.

'This is Inspector Blayne,' Gently told Gabrielle. 'A long while ago we had business together.'

'A long while – aye. And I'm Chief Inspector now, man. But it cannot be business that brings you this way?'

'Not business.'

'Then you'll be for Strathtudlem?'

'Not this time,' Bridget said. 'The Major sold the cottage we had then, and now we've rented one at Kinleary.'

'Aye – Kinleary. It's but a step further on. I'm often that way for a dram at The Clachan. We'll be seein' each other, man, and talkin' over those queer doings up Laggart. You've no' forgotten that ramping hizzie?'

'She isn't easily forgotten,' Gently said.

'Ach, no, man – when you climbed the braes with her, and finished up wi' her dirk at your throat! But are you here for long?'

'For the next fortnight.'

'Then we'll surely be seein' each other again.'

In the car afterwards, as they drove away, Gabrielle turned a thoughtful stare on Gently.

'And shall we be meeting her also – this, what you call, ramping hizzie?'

Smilingly Gently shook his head.

'She is not one of those from your much-coloured past?'

9

'Not one of those. Just a misguided lady who was fell free, as they say here, with a knife.'

'Aha. And for this you admire her?'

'Doubtless for a hizzie she had her points.'

'Then she had better watch out for herself, my friend, because your wife can be a hizzie too.'

They drove on after Geoffrey's Jaguar, through the long, twisty glen that led to Strathtudlem, by the crooked loch, above which rose the ben known locally as the Hill of the Fairies. And that did figure in Gently's much-coloured. He saw Bridget nudge Geoffrey and look back towards their car. But now the pines had almost concealed the 'keeking-stane' where he had climbed with a woman who wasn't Gabrielle. Nevertheless, at the village Geoffrey pulled over, and they got out to renew acquaintance with Maclaren's cottage.

'They've altered it,' Bridget said. 'You'd never take it for the same place. And the hotel. And the store. It doesn't have the same feel at all.'

'The bridge is still there,' Geoffrey said. 'Remember that trek we made up the back road?'

'Oh yes. And George's "guid path" up the braes – but perhaps the less said about that the better.'

Gabrielle looked solemn. She said, 'And it is there that George went with the ramping hizzie?'

'Ahem!' Geoffrey said. 'Something like that. But really, we ought to be getting along.'

It was familiar country now. The Braes of Skilling swept away to their left, then came Loch Cray with the sails of dinghies and the steep pass through Glen Donach; and finally they were cruising down to Kinleary and crossing the bridge by the spreading falls.

'Oh, my dear! And it is here we are staying?'

They paused at the bridge: they couldn't help it. Below them splashed the foaming waters that tumbled by broad sweeps of rock and boulder. The falls were divided by an island, on the tall pines of which jackdaws were cawing. Children climbed on the rocks. Their elders stood watching. Not a passing car but slowed to a crawl.

'And – our cottage?'

Bridget had a sketch map. They followed the Jaguar into Kinleary. At once it made a climbing turn into a road that broke back to run parallel to the falls. And there it waited for them, Fern Cottage, outside the traditional white plaster and slate, inside an agreeable modern conversion, spacious, with every comfort laid on. Geoffrey fetched the key. They hauled in the baggage. They sprawled on chairs in the delectable lounge. And suddenly all the agony of the roads seemed worth it, a paltry price to pay for such contentment.

'That's Ben Lyon, over there!'

From the windows of the lounge stretched a ranging view. Above the descending street of the little town rose a lofty line of rugged hills. The falls were hidden by trees, but they could still hear their distant murmuring. And below the window a ferny rock-garden sank below a terrace, to be reached by steps.

'Well . . . I suppose we'd better get a meal.'

Somehow, they pulled themselves together, chose bedrooms, unpacked, cooked and ate a simple supper. Then – what else? – in the gentle evening they'd strolled back to the bridge and the falls, to wind up at the convenient Clachan and, drink in hand, watch the sun leave the glen. Perfection . . . with even a touch of scandal to colour the moment! A painted lady with her light-of-love, to affront but intrigue Bridget.

'Do you think there's a husband in the background?'

'Oh, come off it, Bridgie!' Geoffrey said. 'They're probably sleeping in separate rooms.'

But Bridget knew a maneater when she saw one.

The next morning they spent desultorily, exploring Kinleary and its shops, though always seeming to wind up at the bridge, the falls and The Clachan. They discovered a guid cake-shop, a useful stores and a post office that was also a bookshop, and – to the professional interest of Gabrielle – an antique shop, housed in an old woollen mill beside the falls.

'This man, he is no fool!'

She had spent an hour appraising his stock. He was a greying, middle-aged man with lined features, whom Gently had noticed

11

at The Clachan the evening before. He had been sitting alone, ignoring everyone, sombrely sipping a glass of lager; but today he was smiling and attentive, seeming to find in Gabrielle a fellow soul.

'He was in Glasgow, he tells me, but, when his wife dies, he moves here. He is an expert in Scottish gem-stones, and sells a great many to American tourists.'

'Did he sell you one?'

'Ha, at those prices? I can buy them cheaper in Rouen.'

Another character was The Clachan's landlord, a sandy-haired man called Hector Menzies. Inevitably, they drifted in there for lunch, and he it was who served them in person. Deftly, he set their plates down. Then he stood staring with narrowed eyes.

'You, man. Have I not seen you before – when I was landlord at The Bonnie Strathtudlem?'

'That was a few years ago,' Gently said.

'A few years – aye, it was. But that was an occasion to be rememberin'. There's you and Alistair Blayne huntin' for the murtherer of Donnie Dunglass – am I no' right?'

'Something of that sort.'

'Aye, I'm with you now,' Menzies said. 'And you're back in these parts, then. But it would not be after the same sort o' thing?'

'Just on vacation.'

'Aye, on vacation. Then I'd best leave you guid souls to your vittles.'

'Wait!' Bridget exclaimed. Menzies hesitated. 'About the couple who were staying here last night,' Bridget said. 'The young man and the lady with the see-through dress. Have they booked in again for tonight?'

Menzies' blue eyes twinkled. 'Not so's you'd notice. Were you after a word with them, then?'

'Just . . . curiosity.'

'Aweel, they've booked out. It was just a one-night stand, you ken.'

'What were their names?'

'I'm not just that certain. But if it is not Smith, then it's likely Jones.'

12

He went off chuckling to himself, and Bridget made a face at his retreating back.

'You are awful, Bridgie,' Geoffrey grinned. 'George, why can't you keep your sister in order?'

'It's too late now,' Gently said. 'She's always been one too many for me.'

After lunch, they had out the maps. Kinleary was sited at the head of Loch Torlinn. A round trip was possible, perhaps forty miles, passing below Ben Lyon on the way. Gabrielle was eager, but Geoffrey and Bridget still felt they'd had driving enough for one while, and in the end it was just the Rover that set off from Fern Cottage.

'Is perhaps the best,' Gabrielle said to Gently. 'Though I like your relatives very much. But to be on our own I like too, and this is our first chance since Friday.'

'Geoffrey wants to be sketching,' Gently said. 'And that's a cue for Bridget to lounge around in the sun.'

So they drove the long miles down the loch to Torlinnhead, with Ben Lyon riding on their flank, and the braes unravelling on the further shore. Behind them Kinleary nestled in a theatre of folding hills, ahead the loch bent through steepening, birch-clad heights. At Torlinnhead they paused for coffee at a hotel that once had claimed Burns as a guest; then they crossed the river which flowed from the loch, and struck the narrow road on the opposite shore.

'This . . . really goes somewhere?'

'The map says it does.'

The road was steep besides being narrow. It climbed by way of hairpins and blind bends, with the ruffled loch sinking rapidly below them. But then they came to a small village, a settlement acknowledged by the map, beyond which the road, though still narrow and bendy, took a more or less level course along the braes. And now the prospect became expansive; the loch spread out below from end to end. Across it loomed the majestic ben and its out-riders, chequered at the lower levels with pine forest and birches. Far away, where the loch ended, one could just make out the smudge of Kinleary, tiny and lost beneath the hills, an insignificant token of man.

'Shall we not stop – just for a few minutes?'

They had arrived at a passing-place more generous than most. Gently eased the Rover into it, and they climbed out to admire that far-ranging view.

'Look – there is the road we came by. And that must be the hotel, back there. But so small! It makes one feel – I do not know. As though one might fly.'

'Perhaps, one day, we could climb the ben.'

'Yes.' Gabrielle snuggled close to Gently. 'Could we not live here, in this place, at least for one whole summer?'

'We can dream of it.'

'Then I shall dream. I will have Fern Cottage placed just here. Each morning I will wake to see this view, and each evening watch the sun go down on it.'

'And when it rains?'

'It won't. My dreams are not so foolish, George Gently.'

But then the idyll was interrupted. A car approached briskly from the direction of Kinleary. A police car: it braked squeakily, and swung into the passing-place ahead of the Rover. A uniform man got out, stood a moment staring at the pair of them; then he approached them.

'If you don't mind, sir, I would like a sight of your licence.'

'My licence?'

'Aye, if you would, sir. It's just a wee check we have on.'

'A check for what?'

'Just your licence, sir. Unless you'd sooner I didn't see it.'

Shaking his head, Gently produced it and handed it to the man. The constable stared at it, his eyes widening, then he hastily handed it back.

'Ach, I'm sorry, sir – no offence! It is just a bit of nonsense we have going.'

'But what sort of nonsense?'

'Ach, just nothing. Nothing to do with the likes of you, sir.'

Whereupon he got back in his car, reversed it jerkily, and sped away.

'Well!'

Gabrielle stared indignantly after the departing car. But Gently only chuckled as he tucked the licence away in his wallet.

'A bit of routine. It sometimes happens.'

'But who did that monkey take us for?'

14

'A wee check, the man said. Perhaps he's hunting for a pair of joy-riders.'

'And we look like that?'

'Or an eloping couple. I had my arm round you when he drove up.'

'Ha,' Gabrielle said. 'I like that better. So now you can put it back again.'

But the mood of the moment had been disturbed, and soon they were back again in the car. The road, as they progressed, sank lower, and the view became correspondingly less spacious. Finally they were threading through woodland and pasture, to emerge, surprisingly, by the car-park of The Clachan.

'Wasn't that another police car, parked in there?'

But Gently had been intent on his driving. However, as he turned into the forecourt of Kinleary's one garage to refill his tank, he observed a third police car, proceeding up the street. The attendant took his money. Gently said:

'Are there always so many police in Kinleary?'

'Ach, no!' The attendant was an untidy fellow with designer-stubble and trailing hair.

'Has something happened?'

'Aye, I'm thinkin'. There was a mannie come here lookin' for his wife. An' she was awa' wi' her fancy fellow, so like there's been ructions hereaboots.'

'What sort of ructions?'

'Na, I can't tell you. But we've had the polis all around here.'

He winked villainously and went to fetch change. Gabrielle exchanged looks with Gently.

'Are you thinking what I am thinking, my friend?'

Gently nodded. 'Bridget's scarlet woman.'

'But is it not likely?'

'More than likely.'

'And, if this husband should have caught up with them?'

Gently shrugged. 'It's not our affair! But it might explain why the constable wanted to see my licence.'

'You mean – he thought we were them?'

'For a passing moment.'

Gabrielle giggled. 'Then I forgive that monkey! I do not wish to be thought a car-thief, but a scarlet woman is another matter. Yet . . . could this be serious?'

Gently shook his head. 'Just a bit of nonsense was what the man said.'

At the cottage they found a meal set and a Bridget anxious in case they should arrive late. Geoffrey, on the other hand, was working on a sketch, which he seemed in no hurry to put aside. He waved an impatient pencil towards them.

'Did you see your friend then, down at The Clachan?'

'My friend?'

'From Balmagussie. The one with a face like Dominie Sampson's.'

'You mean Blayne?' Gently sat down.

'He was here an hour ago,' Geoffrey said. 'Rather disappointed to have missed you. Said you could find him this evening at The Clachan.'

'Was he here on business?'

'I don't think so. Seemed to be amused about something. He was almost at the point of spilling it, then said it would sound better told over a dram. Have you any ideas?'

'Perhaps . . . just one.'

'Oh yes, a very good idea!' Gabrielle said. 'But the good Inspector is right, and it will sound much better over a dram.' She made a swirling gesture before Geoffrey. 'Who do you take me for?' she asked.

Geoffrey stared. 'Who?'

'Would you not take me for a scarlet woman?'

But just then Bridget entered with a dish of hot chops, Geoffrey had to put his sketch-pad away, and the subject of scandal in Kinleary was postponed for a more favourable moment.

When at last, in the cool of the evening, they crossed the bridge and entered The Clachan, they could see no sign of Blayne either in the bar or at the outside tables. However, the landlord winked at them as he set up glasses for a couple of customers, and when he had rung up the payment, lifted the bar-flap and beckoned to them.

'This way. He's in the back parlour – and noo the worse for one or two drams!'

They found Blayne in a small lounge the windows of which overlooked the car-park, and seated with him a sharp-faced man whom Gently recalled as Blayne's former sergeant, Purdy. Purdy was nursing a glass of lemonade, Blayne had an empty whisky-glass before him. On seeing them, Blayne jumped to his feet, almost sending the glass flying.

'Ach, then – you've come! Hector, my mannie, set them up – a dram each for these two gentlemen, and the pretty ladies what they will.'

'Thank you,' Gabrielle said. 'I will also try this, what you say, dram.'

'And you, Bridgie?' Geoffrey grinned.

Bridget glared at him. 'Very well – a dram for me too.'

'Four drams,' Geoffrey said. 'And a refill for our friend here.' He looked at Purdy, but Purdy wistfully shook his head and gestured to the car they could see parked outside.

'Sit ye down,' Blayne said. 'Sit ye down. Ach, the sight of you brings back auld times! I've been chattin' them over with Purdy here, but he's no' the same man without a dram in him.'

'It's the new times we've come to hear about,' Geoffrey said.

'Aye, but every dog in his kennel, Mr Kelling! So sit ye down and bide a wee till Hector fetches in the lubricant.'

They sat, and the drinks came. Geoffrey and Gently raised their glasses. Gabrielle sipped hers with a thoughtful expression. Bridget made a face and set her glass down firmly. Blayne took a hearty pull.

'Ach, it's a guid dram they pour at The Clachan! And noo – and noo, was not Hector tellin' me you were inquiring about the love-birds who stayed here last night?'

'Love-birds indeed!' Bridget snorted. 'A shameless bitch and her toy-boy would better describe them.'

'So you saw them, then?'

'Yes, we saw them.'

'Aye, they made quite an impression,' Blayne said.

'Too much of an impression,' Bridget said.

'Aweel, we must not be uncharitable,' Blayne said. He took another pull at his glass. He looked at Gently. 'This afternoon,' he said. 'You would not have been up Glen Eden, by any chance?'

'Glen Eden?'

'Aye. It's a bit glen that takes off from the other end of the town and runs for miles into nowhere – just a sheep-farm here and there, and some hydroelectric down at this end of it.'

'It sounds a good spot for a picnic,' Gently said.

'You're there, right there, man,' Blayne said. 'Because that's where our love-birds went this morning. On a picnic up Glen Eden. You were not there?'

Gently shook his head.

'A pity,' Blayne said. 'A great pity. A man like yourself. We could not have wanted a better witness on the spot.'

'Has something happened to them, then?'

'I'll tell you the story,' Blayne said. 'They're down in the book by the name of Robertson. But the lady is the wife of a Dr Angus in Glasgow, and her boy-friend a company rep called Fowler. So they're off on a spree, the lady leavin' word that she's visiting her mother in Edinburgh, and this morning they had Hector pack them a picnic, though they didn't let on where they were off to.'

'But – they did tell someone?'

Blayne nodded. 'They inquired the way there at the garage. And it was at the garage, for better or worse, that the lady's husband picked up their trail.'

'This Dr Angus.'

'Aye. Who has a practice out at Bearsden. Who'd been away at a conference down in Durham, and got the truth out o' their domestic when he returned.' Blayne took another pull. 'He's staying in the town, at The Highland Arms down the street – a brisk, pudden'-faced body, who I would not much want to be a doctor of mine.'

'But – did he catch up with them?' Bridget exclaimed.

'Aye – but drink up, drink up!' Blayne grinned. 'You have not touched your glass, Mrs Kelling – and your man is near at the bottom of his.'

With a look of loathing, Bridget snatched up her glass and took a wry sip.

'So,' Blayne said. 'The doctor goes up the glen – and the pity is we cannot turn up a witness. But his own tale is that he comes on Fowler standin' by his car, which is parked on the strath. It's a guid road, you ken, for a few miles, and after that fit only for cattle, but thereabouts is this sonsie spot with a bit of strath to put your car on. Out gets the doctor. – Where is she? he says. – Gone behind a bush, Fowler tells him. And then they have a father and a mother of a row, which ends up with the doctor knocking Fowler down. And all this while the sensible lady is staying behind her bush and keepin' out of it.' Blayne drank.

'What happened then?'

'Why, then Fowler gets in his car and takes off down the glen, and the doctor goes hunting around in the bushes and bawlin' for his missus to show herself.'

'Which – she didn't.'

'No, not she. And I'll tell you what I think happened in a minute. But the doctor, he's gettin' himself in a state, not being able to find hide nor hair of her. It's wild, weary country up there, with a powerful burn running through it, and a lady who took off into that might soon be finding herself in trouble. So the doctor panics and comes flyin' down again, and puts in a report to us that she's missing, and we've been up there, and round about, and havin' a word with the farms in the glen.'

'But no lady.'

'No.'

'So what do you think must have happened?'

'Just this,' Blayne said. 'While those two gowks were rowing, she slips quietly away down the glen.'

'Would that have been possible?'

'Oh aye. I've been over the ground myself. If she kept by the burn she'd be under cover as far as the next bend in the road. And there she'd only to wait for her Lochinvar to pick her up, and away.'

'Does that satisfy the doctor?'

Blayne shook his head. 'Which is why I have patrols watchin' out for them. And why, just for my own satisfaction, I would like to turn up a witness to those jinks up the glen.' He paused to give Gently a shrewd look. 'You're quite sure, man, you were not around there, at about twelve thirty today?'

'Quite sure.'

19

'Ach, well. I'm asking because the doctor says a car went by while they were at it, and then came back again a short while after, like it had been to the road's end, and turned.'

'Can he describe it?'

'Just that it was green. He had his back to the road, you ken.'

'Our own car is gold metallic.'

'Ach, isn't that just the way of things?' Blayne heaved a deep sigh, and rolled his eyes at them. 'Weel, that's the end o' the tale,' he said. 'The guid doctor is waiting to hear the upshot, but he might do better to be traipsin' home to Bearsden. And now I've time for one more glass. Purdy, call that scoundrel Hector. What shall it be, ladies?'

'For me,' Gabrielle said, 'an orange juice. Without ice.'

'Just water,' Bridget said. 'Plain water.'

'Ach, the size of it!' Blayne leered.

2

'George, it's been snowing.'

'Pull the other one.'

'But no – just come and look!'

Incredulously, Gently pushed aside his quilt and felt around for his slippers. They had been late to bed the previous evening. There had been a few more drinks after Blayne had left. The intriguing subject of the doctor's wife had been gone over again from every angle. Maureen – that was her name: they had learned it from the attentive landlord, and that of her boy-friend Darren – 'About what one would have expected!' had been Bridget's tart comment. 'And d'you think the Blayne chiel is right?' the landlord had queried. 'Will she be away now with her fancy?' Bridget had hoped she was stuck up the glen, but the consensus was that Blayne had read it correctly. She had perhaps recognized the approaching car and commanded her boy-friend to keep the doctor busy while she made her escape, and now they were long gone, and assuredly many a mile from Kinleary. So they had wrapped it up, and trailed back to the cottage, and had the maps out over coffee, and voted on a trip to Rannoch Station the next day before, yawning and late, seeking their beds. But now:

'George, it really *is* snow!'

In her dressing-gown, Gabrielle was standing at the window. Gently joined her. From their window they had a prospect over the winding, descending street with, looming over it, the range of great hills that culminated in the 4000-foot peak of the ben. The day was sunny. Swifts squealed over the falls. On a telegraph pole a jackdaw perched, basking. But the hills and the ben were a blank, flat white, as though sugared over by some divine confectioner.

'Is it not strange – yes?'

Gently could only rub his eyes and stare. The effect was unreal. The hills resembled a drawing in line, with all colour removed.

'A Chinese painting, ha?'

'It could be a view in the Himalayas . . .'

Gabrielle giggled. 'I tell you something, my friend. There will be no trip to Rannoch Station today.'

'No trip?'

'You are still asleep. Do you think we shall tear Geoffrey away from all this?'

And so it turned out. At the breakfast table, Geoffrey could scarcely keep his eyes from that view – it was fantastic, it was unbelievable! Surely the god of artists was smiling on him.

'You go. Take Bridget. I can see Rannoch some other day.'

'Oh no,' Bridget said. 'I wasn't keen anyway. Tomorrow will be soon enough for a long trip. This is only Tuesday, remember, and we still have the rest of the fortnight in front of us.'

'And I', Gabrielle said, 'wish to visit the mill again, where that man has a fresh stock of gems coming in. So, that is three to one, George. I think we do not go to Rannoch Station.'

And perhaps even Gently himself was content to while away another day in those delectable surroundings.

After breakfast they separated, Geoffrey to set up his easel on the terrace, Gabrielle to hasten round to the mill, Bridget to stroll down to the shops. Gently walked as far as the post office to pick up a larger-scale map of the district, then sauntered back again to the mill, to find Gabrielle surrounded by trays of cairngorms, amethysts and agates. Parked by the mill was a green Volvo estate. Gently stared at it a moment, then shrugged.

'My dear, you do not come too soon. This man has almost converted me to gem-stones!'

The proprietor, whose name was Collins, smiled apologetically at Gently, and uncovered a fresh tray to reveal lustrous amber.

'Shall it be this brooch – or this?'

'Your wife is a lady of taste,' Collins smiled. 'She has

22

also a keen idea of prices. Is it just possible she is in the trade?'

'Just possible,' Gently said.

'Ah yes,' Collins said. 'One can usually tell. So then a little discount will be called for?'

'I think you may have to make that little a lot.'

In the end, the brooch Gabrielle chose was a cairngorm set in an oval of amethysts, and the price bore small relation to that on the ticket which Collins hastily removed from it. He wrapped it in tissue and found a box for it.

'Are you staying in Kinleary for long?'

'For the fortnight.'

'Ah yes. Your lady tells me you have rented Fern Cottage.' He paused, the box in his hand. 'You will have heard of that odd affair that happened here yesterday. I believe the police are still looking for the couple. You wouldn't have heard if there is any fresh news?'

Gently shook his head.

'A strange business,' Collins said.

Gently said, 'Weren't you at The Clachan on Sunday evening?'

'At The Clachan? I – yes! I did drop in there for a pint.'

'Then you'd have seen the couple.'

'You mean, that was them?'

'They stayed the night at The Clachan.'

'Good lord,' Collins said. 'I suppose I should have guessed. But then, I didn't pay them much attention. Do we – know who they are?'

'The man's name is Fowler.'

'But – the lady?'

'A Mrs Angus.'

'. . . Angus.' He shook his head. 'Well, the names mean nothing to me! And no doubt, when there's any news, it will be all round the town.' He pressed the box into Gabrielle's hand. 'A pleasure,' he said. 'Do call again. I'm expecting another fresh consignment, and it should be here by mid-week.'

'Next time, I will leave my cheque-book at home,' Gabrielle said. 'These gem-stones will be my downfall yet.'

They strolled down to the bridge. Gabrielle looked thoughtful.

'Do you think he did know those people?' she said.

Gently shrugged. 'He certainly seemed interested! But that wouldn't single him out, in Kinleary.'

'Perhaps she was a customer of his, ha?'

'In that case he wouldn't want to admit it.'

'Yes, a customer,' Gabrielle said. 'He perhaps noticed her on Sunday, and now wishes to be certain. Ah me.' She looked at her watch. 'But is it not now time for coffee?'

Yet, for a while, they lingered on the bridge, watching the torrents sweep round the grey rocks, the venturesome children who clambered out on them, the jackdaws that flopped among the pines on the island. Snow there might be on the high hills, but here the June sun was as friendly as ever.

They ordered coffee at The Clachan, and had it fetched to an outside table. As usual, the place was busy, the tables filled with tourists in bright holiday gear. The Clachan was a magnet. It faced the long, narrow bridge, across which vehicles had to crawl among loitering pedestrians, and car after car, when the crossing was accomplished, lingered, paused, then headed for the parking. Their crews tumbled out to queue for drinks, and then joined the others to admire the falls. There was sweat on the brow of the humoursome landlord as he hastened to collect glasses, or dump down a fresh trayful. At last, in a lull, he paused at their table, a wicked twinkle in his eye.

'Have you seen him, then?'

'Seen who?'

'Why, the chiel sittin' over at the far table!'

'Would that be the doctor?'

'Aye, right. With a wee glass before him, fit only for a lady.'

Gently ventured a glance. He caught the angry eye of a bulky man in a black suit. He was seated alone at the most remote table, on which stood a cocktail-glass with a protruding straw.

'The poor man!' Gabrielle murmured. 'One must feel sorry for him, I think.'

'You would not be saying that, lady, if you were standin' here in my shoes.'

'He has been making inquiries?'

24

'Aye, he has. And me rushed almost off my feet. First he'll be for seeing their names in my buik, and then he's all around me with daft questions, and then he's tellin' me – and in front of my company – that I should have known better than taking them in. Man –' Menzies dabbed at his brow – 'it was as well he had bought his drink before he started in on me!'

'Could you answer his questions?'

'Na, na. And maybe I would not if I could. And here's another thing about yon doctor. I had Jock from the garage early on – you ken Jock? He's the scruffy loon who lives in a van at the back of the garage. Well, I'm tellin' him what the Blayne chiel thinks, and all about the row up the glen, and he puts his finger on this – that yon doctor was left alone with the lady. And was he not? Is not Blayne tellin' us? Her fancy takes off, and leaves them together. So maybe the doctor should be a wee less brisk when he's puttin' himself about in Kinleary.'

Gently stared. 'You suspect him of lying?'

'Well, I would not just be saying that! But it stands to his word, and no one else's, and the chiel should be rememberin' that.'

Gently shook his head. 'We have no cause to doubt it, so perhaps you should keep your suspicions to yourself.'

'Oh, aye. But I'm still thinkin'. And if he's at me again I'll maybe throw it up.'

'Meanwhile Inspector Blayne's view is probably the correct one. Mrs Angus was able to rejoin her companion. So the less gossip about it the better – both for your reputation and that of Kinleary.'

'Ach, I'm with you,' Menzies said. 'I'm with you. And now . . . will you be for a refill of coffee?'

The doctor got up and strode away, a dignified figure amongst the tourists. He crossed the bridge without a glance back and turned away into the street.

Gabrielle said, 'I do not know. Perhaps the lady is not so much to blame.'

Gently shrugged. 'It probably wasn't all roses – either on his side or hers!'

'But – you think he tells the truth?'

'I think it the most likely.'

'Yet the good Blayne could not find a witness.'

'That would not be surprising, in such a situation.'

'But still – it could be possible?'

For answer, Gently took out the map he had bought. He unfolded it and spread it out: a 1-inch Survey of Kinleary and district.

'There's your glen.'

The road began at the town-end, by a bridge and a hotel, then wriggled its way along the course of a stream and between closely plotted contours. For about five miles the road was tinted yellow, here and there bounded by hatched lines, but after that became an uncoloured double-hatching that ghosted its way into total wilderness. Farmsteads were few and very far between. At the town-end was a handful of houses. Then there was the hydroelectric installation, straddling the stream, about a mile from the junction.

'My faith . . . do people live in such places?' Gabrielle was gazing at the uncoloured stretch of road.

'Our picnickers wouldn't have gone so far. My guess is they parked their car about here.'

At the end of the coloured section was the junction with a loaning which would offer opportunity for a car to turn, with close by it an expanse of level strath caught in a winding of the stream. And there the road was hatched: as far as maps could tell, a perfect picnic venue.

'And there the lady went behind a bush?'

'Blayne looked it over. It must be credible.'

'And here she is creeping beside the stream?'

'If there was cover I don't see why not.'

Gabrielle shook her head. 'This I tell you, my friend. That lady is no ramping hizzie. Unless there is a good track beside that stream, she is still behind the bush when her boy-friend leaves.'

Gently chuckled. 'We would have to see the spot!'

'And may we not do that, this very afternoon?'

'You mean, a picnic?'

'I say, why not? Because then we can see if the doctor tells the truth.'

Gently brooded over the map. Was it a good idea, or not? In

26

his own mind he felt reasonably certain that Blayne's reading of the event was the correct one. Just this small area of doubt: nothing to back up the husband's account. And certainly the woman was no mountain hizzie if it came to a scramble through rough country . . . At the same time he could imagine Bridget's reaction if, only at the margin, he became involved in this! He folded up the map.

'We'll do it, then. But not a word to Bridget.'

'But if we take a picnic, she must know –'

'Just that we're off out somewhere with a picnic.'

'But if she wishes to come?'

'She won't. And Geoffrey is tied up with his painting.'

'Ah well,' Gabrielle said. 'So drink up your coffee. Already it is late to be going on a picnic.'

Fortunately Bridget had planned a cold lunch, and was quite agreeable to packing them a picnic: pork pie, salad in a bag, and a whole bannock and a thermos of coffee. By twelve thirty they were away and cruising down through the town, past The Highland Arms, in the forecourt of which was parked a pearl-grey Mercedes 320E.

'That is his car?'

It fitted the man, and it was the only car on the forecourt. Gently glanced at the hotel's lounge windows as they passed, but saw only a waiter bearing a tray. And didn't it raise another small question, that the doctor should be hanging on there – knowing himself to be a figure of fun in every bar in Kinleary? His wife had escaped. She was off with her lover. Wherever she was to be sought, it was not here. As Blayne had said, he would be far better off nursing his wrath in polite Bearsden.

'I think he will be finding her at her mother's, yes?'

'At her mother's?'

'Aha.' Gabrielle nodded sagely. 'I think that lady can tell a good lie, and this is how she will handle it now. He has not seen her, yes? It could yet be any woman off with this Fowler. So now he finds her at her mother's, where she said she was going, and ready to shed tears at his dreadful suspicions.'

Gently chuckled. 'You think she could get away with it?'

'But yes. I could, as you say, get away with it myself. He may not believe her, but that is no matter, he has no proof, because he did not see her.'

'The domestic split on her.'

'Ha. A lying jade. I think that domestic is getting the boot.'

'He may have forced an admission from Fowler.'

'Another liar. Who shall believe him?'

'And you think he would swallow that?'

Gabrielle nodded. 'If he is a wise man, he will pretend it. This is the way of husbands and wives who are, perhaps, not very well suited. Is it not so?'

Gently chuckled again. 'And if the good doctor is less than wise?'

'Well then, all tears, she will remain with her mother until he is wiser. Or she is divorced.'

'Which will it be?'

'I think,' Gabrielle said, 'after seeing that doctor, the divorce.'

Now they had turned the bend at the bottom of the street and were passing the outlying houses of the town. Ahead lay a bridge, with beyond it a hotel, and on the left the junction of a minor road.

'This must be it.'

They turned into the road. It ran by the stream that passed under the bridge. Quickly they were leaving the few houses behind and opening a view of level strath and wooded braes. A mile later they reached the small power station, a modest building in pastel brick, and there crossed the stream to plunge into trees on a road that had suddenly become much narrower. It wound with the stream. High banks hemmed it in. At one point the stream came crashing down a fall. Then, at last, the trees thinned, the braes began to withdraw, and they emerged into a broad strath flanked with birch-dotted hills.

'This is not so very wild, ha?'

But they were still on road coloured yellow on the map. An occasional cattle-grid rumbled under their wheels, and they passed a cottage, and later a farm. Gently checked the car's mileometer. Another mile, and they should be at the spot. Ahead, the trees came down to the road, and the stream

28

sheered off, began to lose itself under them. Their goal arrived unexpectedly. The road climbed a minor ridge to a turn amongst trees. And there it lay, just as he had been picturing it, the level apron of strath in the loop of the stream. To make certain, he drove on to the belt of trees beyond, to find, as the map warned, that from thereon the road deteriorated into a track. He came to the loaning, reversed, and drove back. It was perfectly possible to drive off the road and on to the strath. Marks showed that other cars had been there before him: he circled and parked facing down the glen.

'If it was here, my dear, I admire their taste!'

They scrambled out on the sheep-bitten turf. Trees, grey boulders hedged in the stream, and across the road the braes rose in gentle, birch-nursed slopes.

'That may be the bush, yes?'

In fact, the lady had been spoilt for choice. Besides the bush-willow and snowberry that tangled along the bank, there was, unusually, a patch of gorse.

'But if she had been back there –'

'Oh no!' Gabrielle laid a finger on his lips. 'First, we are going to have our picnic – after that, you may play the great detective.'

So the picnic was fetched and laid out, under a birch tree beside the stream, where each had a comfortable boulder to lean against and a perfect view of the ranging braes. They were not without company. Sheep came to inspect them, then ambled off to brood in the shade; rabbits skipped from cover to cover, and a cuckoo landed on a lichen-covered hawthorn. Then:

'What is that little bird?'

A dipper was performing from an overhanging ledge. Black, white, with a touch of red, it gave the impression of an aquatic robin.

'They have named this place truly, my dear. At least, in June, it is an Eden. I no longer care about naughty wives and whether angry husbands are telling fibs.'

'Yet that was why we came here.'

'Oh, pfoo! All that we can leave to the good Blayne. We are on holiday, yes, you and me, and that is all that matters just now.'

29

And Gabrielle stretched out on the soft turf, kicked off her shoes and closed her eyes.

Well, it was that sort of place. Time bid to stand still in the moist-scented air. In a little while Gently, too, was reclining on the turf with closed eyes. One heard the stream, a discontented sheep, the now-distant cuckoo . . . and then . . .?

'My guidness! Can it be you people?'

He came out of the doze he had fallen into with a start. They were no longer alone. Staring down at them, wide-eyed, was a middle-aged lady, supporting a bicycle.

'I – I beg your pardon?'

'If it's you, then I'm tellin' you, you had best be somewhere else. He's up in the town yet, jist waitin' for you to fall into his clutches.'

'He – ?'

'Aye – he's stayin' at The Arms. Whyfore are you comin' back this way?'

Gently shook his head and sat up. 'I think you must be mistaken,' he said.

'Then you're no' that couple? The yins who were up here?'

'No, we're not that couple,' Gently said.

'Ach then, I'm sorry!' The lady looked half-indignant. 'But what was I to think, seein' the pair of you stretched out here? And after the fuss an' bother there's been, wi' the polis up and down, and the phones all ringin'?'

Gently said, 'Do you live in the glen?'

'Aye, where else. I live at Auchtoo.'

'You wouldn't have been this way yesterday?'

'No, I wasna. And more's the pity.'

'You saw nothing of what happened.'

'Not me. But it's all round the toon this mornin'. And that doctor loon is rampin' around there, waitin' for the polis to get their hands on them. And you're sure you're not them?'

'Quite sure.'

'I wouldna be blamin' you, you ken. But if you're no', then I'm sorry I bothered you, and I'll jist be pedlin' back up the glen.'

And with great dignity she wheeled her bike to the road, jerked herself on the saddle, and rode away.

'Oh, my dear!' Gabrielle had scarcely been able to restrain her

30

laughter. 'And this is the second time it happens – who shall say now I am not a scarlet woman?'

'Perhaps we should have had Bridget along for a chaperon.'

'Oh no, but that would spoil the fun. And in this place which is so romantic, who knows? It may happen to us again and again.'

'In that case, we had better explore the escape route.'

'Oh, that is for polis-men, like Blayne.'

'Still . . . since we are here?'

Gabrielle shook her hair. 'Very well. Because it may be this lady will need a bush too.'

Gently paused. 'And if you did?'

'Ha?'

'If you wanted a bush, which one would you choose?'

'If I wanted . . .?' Gabrielle looked about her. 'I think, those gorses. They are the most polite.'

Gently nodded. 'But if Mrs Angus used them, she could hardly have escaped along the bank. And just here she would have had to remain squatting if she were to avoid being seen by her husband.'

'So this she does, why not?'

Gently shook his head. 'Just a point! Also, she may not have had to disturb the sheep, which today are lying there in the shade.'

'Oh, these detectives!' Gabrielle said. 'I am thinking, next time, I shall invite Geoffrey.'

They tidied up the remains of the picnic and then set out to explore the bank. Blayne's theory was credible. Boulders, bushes, alders and willows provided cover sufficient for a cautious retreat. The sheep had to be roused – they galloped out on the strath, but on the previous day they might have been elsewhere; and here and there gaps occurred in the cover where the fugitive would have had to crouch and choose her moment. But the theory was credible. The ground was rock or thick moss, silent to the step. Once or twice Gently came upon partial footprints, but whether the lady's or Blayne's it was impossible to tell. There were also hoof-prints of the sheep, and larger ones, which may have been a deer's. Finally, within three hundred yards, the stream passed by the ridge where the road made its turn, and where trees rendered further caution unnecessary. They came out on the road at a point completely screened from any watcher below.

'Now,' Gabrielle said. 'The great man is convinced?'

'It fits,' Gently admitted. 'Just about.'

'Ha,' Gabrielle said. 'I can see it all. Here the lady is waiting, with her heart in her mouth. Will he get away, her handsome young lover, or will her husband have wreaked a fatal revenge? She hears a car start, but which one? Here she hides, behind this boulder. The car arrives. It is him, it is him! He brakes, she runs out, runs round the car and jumps in. Away – away! But where? To my mother's at Edinburgh I must go! He has not seen me, I can face it out, but – to Edinburgh, before he shall get there!'

Gently laughed outright. 'Perhaps something like that!'

'And now, we get back to our holiday, yes? For two lovers we are not behaving well. As yet, not once have you kissed me, George Gently.'

They returned to the strath, where the sheep eyed them resentfully. Gabrielle stretched out again beside the stream. But the gorse remained to be explored, and after a moment's hesitation, Gently strolled over towards it.

'You wish to be alone?' Gabrielle called.

Gently shrugged, but didn't answer. The gorse extended a formidable barrier at the foot of the trees that hid the loaning. Yes, it was a much better prospect for a lady seeking her privacy. It could be entered from either side, from the road or from the bank of the stream. At once there was thick cover, but permitting glimpses of the strath besides . . . it was only that, between it and cover down the bank, existed a gap of some twenty yards. Gently strolled among the bushes, surprised a rabbit, and found the hoof-marks of sheep. But nothing else. Plainly, the lady had chosen the snowberry and the alders.

'George, you are to sit down with me. How else shall people take us for runaway lovers?'

In fact, the up-the-glen woman with the bicycle was the only other person they had seen. It was the same in the hour that followed: the sheep, the distant cuckoo were all. For runaway lovers, or even others, that spot in Glen Eden was ideal. At last Gently stirred and sat up.

'Any longer, and we shall be late for tea!'

Regretfully, they packed the picnic gear in the boot of the Rover and set off back down the glen. The glen, which that morning had been lines on a map, but which now seemed to belong to them, a familiar place. Again the cattle-grids rumbled under their wheels, they passed the farmstead and the cottage, again entered the trees in the ravine, slowed as they passed the grumbling torrent. Then, they were crossing the bridge by the power station: and suddenly Gabrielle caught Gently's arm.

'My dear – are not those police cars?'

Four patrol cars were parked on the apron in front of the station. Gently slowed, and as he did so an ambulance came racing round the bend to turn in front of them. At that moment a uniform man came out of the building, followed by a familiar, lanky figure; the latter paused to stare at the Rover, then came running and waving them to stop. Gently pulled over and let down his window. Blayne came panting up beside them.

'Man, I can use you! Can you spare me five minutes?'

'If I can be of any assistance.'

'Aye, you can! I'm in need of a mannie who has seen Mrs Angus, and will know her again.'

'But wouldn't Dr Angus – ?'

'No, I'm tellin' you! It's an independent testament that I'm wanting. So if your bonnie lady would not mind –'

'But what's happened? Have you found her?'

'Ach!' Blayne glanced at Gabrielle. 'But it will be over the papers tomorrow, so I may as well be tellin' it now. Aye, we've found her, if it's her. She wound up against the grid of the hydro electric.'

'You mean – she was drowned?'

Blayne turned away. 'The poor fulish soul,' he said. 'She was strangled.'

33

3

'Strangled . . .!' Gabrielle was gazing at Blayne with horrified eyes. 'But this is sure?'

'Aye, I'm feared so. We have the surgeon with her now.'

'And it is she? This Mrs Angus?'

'I cannot think who else it will be. But your man can perhaps tell us for certain – he is not one that forgets a face.'

'But . . . did she not escape?'

'That's a' by the board now. We're dealin' with a different kettle of fish. And I'm wishful to be certain where I stand before the doctor gets here. He's on his way.'

'But I saw her too!'

Blayne shook his long skull. 'I would not be asking it of you, lady. Your man is all I need. It is not a pretty sight in there.'

'But – !'

Gently climbed out of the car. 'You drive back to the cottage,' he said. 'Tell them not to wait tea, and that I'll be back there as soon as I can.'

'Oh George, this is terrible! And all this while –'

'The Inspector will find me transport.'

'We were making fun, and thinking –'

'Just get along now. And make my apologies to Bridget.'

Gabrielle sniffed and wiped her eyes. Then she scrambled into the driving seat. Gently kissed her; she clung to him for an instant. Then she fastened her seat-belt and drove away. Blayne sucked air through his teeth.

'As weel,' he said. 'As weel. It's no' just the strangling marks on that body, and I'm hoping there's enough of the face left for you to recognize.'

34

'The face has been battered?'

'Aye. Though the surgeon says the injuries are post-mortem. We're thinking they happened on the way down here, when the body came slammin' over the falls.'

'He gives an ETD?'

'Above twenty-four hours.'

'Time enough?'

Blayne nodded sombrely. 'If she went in there around noon yesterday, she'd arrive here about now, so the manager reckons.'

They stared at each other.

'Let's get in.'

Blayne led the way into the building. They passed through a hall, between grumbling generators, and entered what appeared to be a store-room. There the two ambulance men stood by with a stretcher, and the police surgeon was snapping shut his bag. He said:

'I've tidied the face up as well as I could, but don't blame me if it won't pass muster. I've ascertained that there's been recent dental work, so at a pinch we can fall back on that.'

'Fine, just fine,' Blayne said. 'And I've a mannie here who kens the lady we're thinkin' of.'

'Then he'd better prepare himself,' the surgeon said. 'This isn't an encounter I would wish on anyone.'

The body lay covered with a plastic sheet, and abruptly the surgeon stooped and drew it back. What lay beneath seemed, at first sight, to be only a grotesque caricature of a human face. Gently steeled himself to examine it. At one side the jaw-bone protruded through the flesh. The nose was askew, the eyes protruding, the forehead laid open by a vicious gash; and on the neck were the tell-tale bruises of what must have been a violent strangulation. But . . . the identity of that face? Perhaps it was the tangled black hair that helped him. Dulled with mud and matted with weed, still it suggested the woman he had seen. And then, slowly, the rest began to fall into place, the eyes retreating, the nose straightening, the pallid lips drawing into shape.

'To the best of my belief, this is Mrs Angus.'

'Ach!' Blayne sighed. 'Then we're in business. But I was

35

dooms certain before. There could not have been another such taken from the burn.'

'I won't ask for particulars,' the surgeon said. 'But you can take it as read that this is homicide. Just get the body along to me.' And he drew the sheet back over the ruined face.

At that point, Purdy hastened in. 'We have Dr Angus waiting outside, sir!'

'Have we, now,' Blayne said. He looked at Gently. 'Shall we be for having him in?'

After a pause, Gently nodded.

'I'll be going,' the surgeon said.

'Na, hang about, will you,' Blayne said. 'It may be this chiel will be requiring your services.'

It was as well.

Angus strode in with pale face but with flaming eyes. He paused to glare at Blayne, at the surgeon, at Gently; then his eyes fell on the sheeted figure. He pushed past them and dropped beside it. He ripped the sheet back from the face. He stared and stared with bulging eyes. Then groaned, and keeled over in a dead faint.

'Something – that box! – to stick under his feet!'

The surgeon had laid Angus flat on the floor. Under his head he had shoved the medical bag, under his feet a carton pulled from a shelf. Then he wrestled with the doctor's bow-tie, and unbuttoned the top of his shirt.

'Will he be needing a dram?'

'Good lord, no! Unless you want him retching over the floor. Just give him air. Is he connected with the lady?'

'Aye, you might say so,' Blayne said.

'In that case, perhaps these two gentlemen should get on with the job they've come to do.'

Obediently, the two ambulance men unstrapped their stretcher and laid it down beside the body; but just as they were about to lift the body, Angus came to himself with a start.

'Wait!'

He kicked the carton aside and dragged himself to his feet. 'Easy now!' the surgeon admonished him, but Angus paid him no attention. Shakily, he drew back the sheet again, stared again at those ghastly features. It was impossible to read his pallid face or any expression in the empty eyes. Finally he drew himself up straight, signalled the ambulance men to continue. Blayne looked at Gently, who shrugged.

'Should you not be sittin' down, now?' Blayne said to Angus.

'I would recommend it,' the surgeon said.

Angus glared at both of them, but didn't sit down. Instead, he stood, trembling slightly, watching the ambulance men loading the stretcher, and when it was done, signalled again, for them to carry the body out. The surgeon decided to leave too, after another sharp glance at Angus. Then they were left alone with the doctor, and a damp patch on the store-room floor. Blayne jiffled a little.

'You'll be havin' no doubts, then. That was your lady who was under the sheet?'

'That was Maureen.' He had a hard, clipped voice and drew his head back as he spoke.

'And you being a doctor and a' that –'

'You don't have to tell me how she died. Or when. Or where. And I can hazard a guess at the post-mortem injuries.'

'Aye, weel, then.' Blayne rocked his shoulders. 'I'll not have to be tellin' a man like yourself. It's a queerish business, what happened yon, and a few questions will need to be answered.'

'On the contrary. Nothing could be plainer.'

'Aweel, I can understand you thinking so. But from the point o' view of the Perthshire Constabulary, there's matters we shall have to be going into.'

'Just one. And that's the whereabouts of Maureen's killer.'

'You mean the chiel Fowler?'

'Who else? I trust the search for him is in progress.'

'Aye, it is, it is.' Blayne's shoulders moved again. 'And some short, sharp answers we'll be wantin' from him. But you'll ken this – a man like you – that it's queer he should be liftin' his hand against the lady. Now whyfore would he?'

'He seduced her, didn't he?'

'But that's no call to put his hands round her throat.'

'But for heaven's sake, man! Who else could have done it?'

'We'll be askin',' Blayne said. 'We'll be askin'.'

37

'Good God!' Angus towered over Blayne, and there was no pallor in his cheeks now. 'Am I to believe – to believe for one moment – that you suspect me of the murder of my wife?'

'Ach, I'm not sayin' that, Blayne said. 'It's still a' in the pot as yet, you ken. But we have to be lookin' hither and yon, and putting together what we've got.'

'But I never set eyes on my wife yesterday!'

'That's in your statement,' Blayne said. 'I have it in the car.'

'And it's the truth!'

'FIne,' Blayne said. 'Fine. It's just a pity the chiel Fowler won't be able to confirm that. You're sayin' he was away.'

'But I told you the truth.'

Blayne wagged his head. 'But a man like you must be seein' our predicament. Here's the husband of this lady left there alone with her, and him in a taking about her misbehavings. He's tellin' us true, he says – and we have no evidence for doubting it. But still it's a pity the chiel Fowler took off, and left just you there, with never a witness.'

'There was this car!'

'So there was, so there was. But that was back down the glen ahead of Fowler.'

'But the driver could testify that my wife wasn't with us.'

'Aye, when we find him. If ever we do.'

'You mean – that isn't good enough?'

'I'm meanin' just this.' Blayne surveyed the doctor with narrowed eyes. 'Maybe it's true, and maybe it's not, that we'll have it tied up when we nab Fowler. Till then we'll be pushin' our inquiries and weighing this thing with that. And man, you're in the middle of this, so I'll be wantin' you where I can lay my hands on you. And you'll be stayin' on at The Highland, at least till we're getting a grip on Fowler.'

Angus glared at him. 'But how can I help you?'

Blayne slid a look at Gently. 'I'm thinkin',' he said. 'Maybe a wee trip up the glen. Just to get it right clear in my mind, what you've been tellin' me in your statement.'

'You wish me to take part in a reconstruction?'

'Ach, the very word!' Blayne said. 'And I ken this gentleman has been lookin' the ground over, so perhaps he'll oblige us with his company too.'

38

Angus's glare switched to Gently. 'And who might this gentleman be?' he snapped.

'You would not need to be askin' that,' Blayne grinned. 'If you were just twa steps over the border.'

Three police cars made the trip. Angus was placed in the custody of Purdy. The sun was yet high above the braes and the narrow road as empty as ever. As they passed the falls, Blayne slowed the car to stare at the dashing waters, then hissed air through his teeth and accelerated after the others. They passed the cottage, then the farm, and finally mounted the ridge and eased down to the strath. The three cars parked in a line close to where the Rover had parked earlier.

'Can you remember, now, how it was yesterday . . .?'

Abruptly, Angus pointed to the spot where the red Sierra had stood. One of the police cars was manoeuvred on to it, and parked facing down the glen, as the doctor directed.

'And your bonnie Mercedes?'

A second police car was reversed into that position.

'Now – when you were comin' over the hill. Where was the laddie when you first caught sight of him?'

He had been lounging by his car, Angus said, with his back to the road, but had turned quickly at the sound of the approaching vehicle.

'He was lookin' towards the bushes?'

'He may have been.'

'But you caught not any sight of the lady?'

Angus bit his lips tight.

'Aweel,' Blayne said. 'So then he hears your car. What then?'

'He knows my car. We've done business with him. For a moment I thought he was going to run. Then he stood grinning by his car, all ready to brazen it out.'

'And still no sight of the lady?'

Angus gave him an evil look.

'I'm thinkin',' Blayne said, 'that hearin' the car stop, she may have popped her head up to see who it was.'

Angus stared at the braes.

39

'So then she didna,' Blayne said. 'There's just you and the laddie. We'll take it from there.'

After a pause, Angus said, 'I got out of my car. I walked across to him. I stared him in the eyes. I said, "All right, then. Where is she?" And he said, "She's just gone behind a bush." And he was grinning as though he thought it was all a joke.'

'Did he point to any particular bush?'

'As I recall it, no he didn't.'

'Just a wee nod?' Blayne imitated the gesture.

'I recall nothing of the sort at all. However, just then I called to her to come out, and automatically I looked towards those gorses. So did he. But when I searched them later I could find no sign that she had been there.'

'You did not go charging in there, then?'

'I did not,' Angus said icily. 'If you must know, I felt that Maureen could wait. I had her seducer to deal with first. He stood there grinning like the clown he was. And something snapped. I knocked him down.'

'Did you then,' Blayne said. 'And something snapped, I think you said.'

'Yes.' Angus stared at him bitingly. 'And you may make what you like of that.'

'Just so,' Blayne said. 'Let's get on.'

Angus jerked his head back. He continued to stare. 'Fowler scrambled up. He dodged round the car. He said something like, "That wasn't necessary at all." And then he had the impudence to tell me that I knew he wasn't the first, and that I was lucky she hadn't left me years ago. I demanded to know what he meant. He claimed she had told him some scandalous stories. He was kind enough to remind me that she'd been married when I met her, and even suggested she had been a patient of mine.'

'But she was not?'

'No. She was not.'

'But there was a divorce, like?'

'She divorced him.'

'And then . . . she was takin' up with you?'

Angus said furiously, 'I will not discuss that!'

'What I'm thinkin' is,' Blayne said, 'perhaps the laddie had a point, and the lady was unco easy in her ways. And just maybe you were not that ignorant of her manner o' carrying on.'

'I said, I will not discuss that! Those are the slanders that Fowler threw at me. He claimed I was aware that Maureen had lovers, and that a sensible course would be for me to close my eyes to it.' Angus breathed a little faster. 'I believe I disabused him. I insisted that he should retire. I advised him that it was useless for him to remain there, because Maureen would be returning with me. I was even foolish enough –' Angus ground his teeth – 'to proffer an apology for that moment of violence. And the upshot was he got back in his car and drove off down the glen.'

'Fine,' Blayne said. 'Fine. I'm gettin' the hang o' it. And all this time, no glim of the lady. But we're forgetting this car you say came by while you were arguing it out with the laddie.'

'There was such a car. I can tell you no more.'

'But about when would it be passin', now?'

Angus stared for an instant. 'To my recollection, when Fowler was picking himself up from the ground.'

'Aye. So like the driver would have seen you strike him.'

'Regrettably, I have to admit it.'

'And he did not stop, or slow down like?'

'He did not. He drove on.'

Blayne nodded. 'And when he came back again – what would be the state o' play then?'

'We were disputing. On either side of the car. It could not have been much more than five minutes later.'

'So he sees you disputin', and keeps going.'

'I cannot imagine him wishing to intervene.'

'And the colour of the vehicle was green – you cannot add to that?'

Angus pointed to the stand-in car. 'I was standing on this side of it. With my back towards the road.'

'Aye,' Blayne said. 'A pity. But maybe we'll catch up with the driver yet. And now we've got Fowler goin' back down the glen. Let's be hearing what happened after that.'

Angus stared at the car, his mouth bitter. 'What happened I gave exactly in my statement. I called for Maureen to show herself, adding that her boy-friend had taken himself off.'

41

'And then?'

'I searched for her.'

'Keep goin'.'

'Very well. I first searched those gorses. They seemed the obvious place, and it may be I got the impression she was there from Fowler. I kept calling. I didn't find her. I penetrated into the trees. Then I came back along the bank and searched as far as the bend in the road. She wasn't there either. She wasn't down the road. I returned to my car. I kept calling.'

'And all this time – no sight of her?'

His face was grim. 'No sight. No sound.'

'Yet she could not have been far.'

He turned away. The knuckles of his hands were showing white.

'You've nothing to add, now?'

'Yes – just this!' Angus turned on Blayne, his plump face working. 'You were saying that Fowler could have no reason for doing what he must have done to my wife. But I – I can guess at a reason – because I have been her husband for thirteen years! And I can tell you that Maureen was a mistress of provocation, of calculated mockery and scorn. She took delight in it. She stopped at nothing. She could be as foul-mouthed as a woman of the slums. I should not be speaking this of the dead, but you drive me to it in my own defence.'

'Weel, weel,' Blayne said. 'This is interesting.' He slid Gently a sly look. 'And you're saying she could have played these tricks on Fowler – and maybe something snapped wi' him, too?'

'Yes, I do say it. And I scorn your imputation.'

'Just passin' through my mind,' Blayne said. 'With such a woman all things are possible. But you'll be the judge. After thirteen years.'

'Are you offering to accuse me?'

'Jings, no!' Blayne said. 'Not without a deal more than is showin' yet. So we'll just get on and give the place a look-over, in case there was something we were missing yesterday.'

He summoned the men and appointed them, some to search the gorses, some the bank. Angus looked on, a discordant figure in his black business-suit and ruffled tie. Blayne accompanied his men. Gently stood at a distance. At last Angus moved to a

42

boulder and sat down. Slowly his head dropped, little by little; and then he covered his face with his hands.

The search was a mere formality, and soon the three cars were proceeding back down the glen. Blayne drove in silence till they drew level with the farmstead and their wheels were drumming over its grid. Then he heaved a feeling sigh.

'So what's your opinion of the doctor, man?' he asked.

Gently kept his eye on the distant peaks, from which the previous night's dusting of snow had almost vanished. He said:

'The Doctor is in an awkward situation.'

'Aye, I ken that fine! But is it him we're lookin' at, now? Because you've been watching a' like an auld hoodie, and I'm thinking you're half-way into this business.'

'Perhaps you should be asking me my opinion of Fowler.'

'Ach, I'm almost feeling sorry for that laddie!'

Gently nodded. 'But until you find him, it might be best to hold your fire. Against the doctor there is opportunity, but so far not much else. And if it should happen he's telling the truth, then the odds are stacked against Fowler.'

'Aye, I see that.' Blayne sucked air. 'It may be just my prejudice about yon doctor. What we're wantin' now is a bonnie witness, one who can tip the scales this way or that.'

'You'll have checked on the car he says he saw.'

'I did. There's but three of that colour in the town.'

'I noticed a green Volvo estate outside the antique shop.'

Blayne nodded. ''Tis the chiel Collins' bus. It was in the garage yesterday for new plugs and an oil-change, while the other twain were at Balma' and Stirling.'

'No luck at the farmstead?'

'You ken it stands back. I was hoping for more from this cottage we're passin'. It belongs to a painter laddie called McDermid, and those windows you're looking at are those of his studio.'

'He could tell you nothing?'

'He was not there, man! I'm told he's in Edinburgh, settin' up an exhibition. And the hydro electric was not watching cars, though I've still to try the houses lower down.'

43

Gently said, 'That driver could be a vital witness. From where he turned the car he could see the back of the gorses. If he saw Mrs Angus there then we're looking at the doctor. If he didn't we're looking at Fowler.'

'Ach, and suppose he's just another visitor, and scared off by the row he found goin' on there? We could ask and put it about, but I doubt if that laddie will be coming forward.'

'Then we're left with no witness. And Fowler.'

'Aye.' Blayne glimpsed at the falls they were passing, and flinched. 'And the longer we are layin' hands on him, the more I'll be leaning that way. For why would he be goin' off like that? It cannot be just that he was scared of Angus. And he has not gone home – I've been on to Glasgow. He is not actin' the part of an innocent laddie.'

'Though . . . if he didn't know?'

Blayne sighed again. 'Then I'll be praying for the luck o' a good policeman! And thanking a colleague, if so I may call you, for givin' me his countenance up the glen.'

They came to the power station. Blayne drove on, past the junction and through the town. Children were still perching on the rocks of the fall, their elders still lounging at the tables of The Clachan. Blayne halted at the cottage, where Rover and Jaguar were drawn up together on the paved forecourt.

'Will you come in?'

Blayne shook his head. 'I'm thinking your lady may not wish my company. So I'll just be thanking you again, and goin' about my bit business.'

Gently watched him turn, wave and drive away. Then the cottage door opened, and Gabrielle was beside him. Her eyes were large. She said:

'Was it her, then? The scarlet woman?'

Gently nodded.

'Oh, my dear!' She clutched his arm, and her hand was trembling.

'First, you had better have your tea. We can talk about this later.'

As usual, Bridget was common-sense in person, and she had

44

a pot of tea brewed before Gently was well-nigh through the door. A corner of the table was still set, and rissoles were warm under the grill: she sat him down, brought his plate in, and set a cup of tea beside it. Then she poured cups for the others. Gently said:

'I'm sorry, Bridget.'

Bridget sniffed. 'And so you should be. Though I suppose you couldn't help it.'

'Oh, come on Bridgie!' Geoffrey said. 'They might have roped in any one of us. We all saw her at The Clachan. It was just George's bad luck that he was passing.'

'Eat your tea,' Bridget said. 'It wasn't just bad luck that George was out there.'

'Well, he wasn't meaning to get caught up with it. You will have to blame friend Blayne for that.'

Bridget sipped tea for a while. She said, 'I suppose it really was that woman?'

Gently nodded.

'And she – ?'

'I expect Gabrielle will have told you.'

In spite of herself, Bridget shuddered. She took several more sips. She said, 'Well, she probably deserved it. And there's no reason why we should feel guilty.'

Geoffrey said, '*Were* you feeling guilty?'

'Shut up, Geoffrey,' Bridget said.

'I, I am feeling guilty,' Gabrielle said. 'But that is because we make these jokes – while all the time this poor lady is dead.'

'We,' Bridget said, 'were not to know that. We spoke about the woman as we found her. I'm sorry, and I wish it hadn't happened, but I don't see why we should let it spoil our holiday.' She darted a quick look at Gently. 'You haven't let yourself in for anything, have you?'

Gently mumbled through a mouthful.

'I take that to mean no,' Bridget said. 'Of course, if your presence is indispensable, that's another thing again. But it seems to me you have made your contribution, and now it can be left to the appropriate authority.'

'Blayne,' Geoffrey grinned. 'But hold on, Bridget! I want to do a portrait of that weird physog.'

Bridget dealt him a steely glance. 'I think that can wait for another occasion. In the meantime our plan for tomorrow was an excursion to Rannoch Station, and unless the heavens descend I propose we stick to that.'

There was no dissentient voice. Gently finished his meal and drank his tea. By then the sun was casting long shadows and the jackdaws seeking their pines on the island, which clearly made it time for a saunter to The Clachan and for the drinking of a sundowner at an outside table.

'That sister of yours,' Gabrielle murmured, as she and Gently paused once more to gaze at the falls. 'She is of strong character, yes? But I think, all the same, she is a little ashamed.'

'Perhaps. A little.'

'Yes.' Gabrielle stared at the rushing water. 'But, for myself, I cannot help thinking of that poor lady, once so full of life.'

4

Alas for Bridget's good intentions, there was no escaping the topic of the tragedy at The Clachan. Rather, the news of it, after running round the town, had washed up here as at a natural point of focus. The tables were a-buzz with it. Eyes covertly observed them. Clearly Gently's part in the event had got abroad. For a moment it seemed that Bridget might cancel the visit, but then she strode frigidly to the most distant table, and took the chair with its back to that impertinent company.

'You had better get in the drinks, George. And be good enough not to hang about gossiping.'

Easier said than done! When Gently entered the crowded bar, he was immediately grabbed by the excited landlord. A whisky was pushed into his hand, and a seat at the bar instantly made for him.

'The Blayne chiel was here – it's a' around! He's sayin' it was not altogether just a drownin', like. And yon doctor and a' – and yourself – ach, there's been nothin' like it here for a wee while! And you're sayin' it was her? There's no doubt?'

'I came in to order drinks –'

'Aye – on the house, on the house! But is it a fact – she's the doctor's lady?'

Gently hesitated, but what was the use? 'The victim is identified as Mrs Angus.'

'Ach, then it's true – it's her – it's her!' He sent a triumphant look round the cluster of gazing faces. 'And the Blayne chiel is for callin' you in – and you're lookin' her over, and then gangin' up the glen. And the doctor with you – man, I would not want to be in his shoes tonight! And you'll be tellin' us?'

Gently stared at him. He said, 'One thing I'll be telling you.'

'Aye?'

'I'll be telling you not to jump to conclusions, and to wait for the investigation to take its course.'

'Ach, but man!'

Gently stared at the company. 'Unless, that is, anyone here can help the inquiry. And then they should take their information to the police. Because I have no official connection with the case.'

'But man – man!'

'Now I'd like to order.'

A sudden silence had struck the gathering. Here and there, one or two of the drinkers began inconspicuously to edge away. The landlord gazed at them. He gazed at Gently.

'But you cannot just shog it off that way, man! You're right – aye, you're right – it becomes a man like yourself to take a line. But the lady was here, at my own hotel, and we'll be for knowin' the ins and outs o' the matter. Is not that fair?'

'If I may just order.'

'But there's things you might be hearin', too – from myself, who had words with yon doctor – and Jock here, who saw him off up the glen.'

'Ach, not I, Hector – it was the boss!' The assistant from the garage shook his greasy locks. 'I was nearby, but the boss dealt wi' him. He kent the young laddie had asked for the glen.'

'But you were tellin' us –'

'I was nearby. I heard the way yon doctor was ravin'. An' I was sayin', an' I'll say it again, I'm no' that surprised at the way things turned out.'

'But you dealt with the laddie, did you no'?'

'Ach, he was a douce, harmless body. He gave me a pund over the charge, just for tellin' him about the glen.'

'And you're no' surprised, you're sayin'?'

The assistant stroked his greying stubble, and eyed Gently. 'I'll be havin' my opinion, no doubt. An' maybe it's that o' a few other people.'

'Aye, and I'm thinkin' it's the Blayne chiel's for one.' The landlord turned again to Gently. 'So will you not be givin'

48

us just a wee hint – just a nod – about the way the wind is blowin'?'

Gently said, 'Another whisky. A gin and lime. And a lime and soda.'

'Ach – but there'll be no harm in it!'

'Just the drinks,' Gently said. 'Start pouring.'

But when he got back outside with the drinks on a tray, it was to find their table similarly invested. The antique dealer, Collins, had drawn up a chair, and was holding forth to a grim-faced Bridget. Seeing Gently, he rose apologetically.

'Sorry – forgive me! – but I had to talk to someone. I heard of this terrible business from a customer, and it's been preying on my mind.'

Gently shrugged. 'But you didn't know the lady.'

'That's just the point – I think I did! I knew her face was vaguely familiar, and after we'd talked about it this morning I suddenly remembered . . .'

Gently dealt out the drinks and took his seat at the table. Bridget said waspishly, 'You took your time,' and Geoffrey was grinning as he picked up his glass. Gabrielle was looking grave. Collins sat himself again. He said:

'A lustre jug. I remember it quite plainly. It was . . . a few years ago, now. And I had to accept the lady's cheque.'

'Did it bounce?' Geoffrey grinned.

'No, of course it didn't bounce! But you have to be extremely careful when you accept a cheque from an unknown customer.'

'Thank you, monsieur,' Gabrielle said. 'That I must take to be a compliment.'

'But that's just what I mean!' Collins spread his hands. 'One has to be a pretty good judge of character. With Mrs Gently I could feel there was no problem. And it was the same with poor Mrs Angus.'

Bridget sniffed. 'I wouldn't have trusted her.'

'Ah, but you hadn't talked to her,' Collins said. 'In the course of the deal we had a lengthy conversation, and she struck me as a person of integrity.'

'But not, it seems, where her husband was concerned.'

Collins tried to smile, but the smile wouldn't come. He turned to Gently. 'But perhaps you can tell me – they say

49

you were out there – whether the poor lady had to suffer very much?'

Gently sipped his drink. 'Perhaps not much.'

'It was . . . quick?'

Gently said nothing. Collins stared at his hands. He said: 'And – the husband?'

'What about him?'

'Oh, nothing. It was just that I heard . . .'

Gently said, 'Dr Angus is assisting the police. So also will be the young man, Fowler. Until the latter person is contacted there is nothing else to be said about the matter.'

'Then, as yet . . .?'

'The matter is under investigation.'

Collins didn't catch his eye. 'It's so terrible,' he said. 'A person one has known, and who one has seen again recently. And a customer too. Terrible.'

'No more lustre jugs,' Geoffrey said.

Collins didn't seem to hear him. After a few more moments he rose, excused himself, and set off towards the town.

They sat for a while in silence, listening to the falls, watching the sun slide behind its hill, hearing the chatter from neighbouring tables, a subdued rhythm from the juke-box in the bar. At last the sun went, and Bridget rose.

'Well, if we're going on that trip tomorrow . . .'

On the stroll back, Gabrielle hugged Gently's arm. Bridget strode ahead. Geoffrey trailed a step behind her.

'Rain.'

The previous morning had brought its vision of snow-dusted peaks, but today, when Gently went to peer at the window, the peaks were shrouded in heavy wrack. Rain glimmered on the slate roofs below and pattered on the terrace under the window, while the distant murmur of the falls had taken on a deeper, more urgent note. But Bridget was undaunted.

'It can't last all day, and anyway it's the sort of weather for Rannoch.'

'This Rannoch,' Gabrielle said doubtfully. 'What is it?'

'It's a moor. The most famous moor in Scotland.'

'It is very large?'

'Very. And full of bogs and pools called lochans.'

'And one should see this in rain?'

'Of course,' Geoffrey said. 'Snow might be better, but rain will do. Unless you're soaked or frozen to the bone, you can't appreciate the true mood of Rannoch.'

'And this – we do?'

'Better ask Bridget.'

'Oh, stop talking nonsense!' Bridget said. 'Geoffrey, we shall have to stop in the town to buy bread. And while I'm doing that you can pick up some fruit.'

It was nearly ten when they got away, but by then the rain had faded to a mizzle. They passed several patrol cars parked outside the police station, and the doctor's Mercedes still occupied its forecourt. Gabrielle glanced at Gently as they went by.

'You think, by now, they have caught the young man?'

'Perhaps.'

'You wish to stop and ask?'

Gently shook his head firmly. 'We'll leave it with Blayne.'

'But . . . you have ideas?'

Gently shook his head again. 'Nothing that Blayne won't have thought of too. So we'll just play fair, and stick with Bridget. And keep our minds on Rannoch Moor.'

'Then, if you say so,' Gabrielle said. But she couldn't help looking back at the parked cars.

Jaguar and Rover, they pursued the stretching road by the loch and the ben, the reaches of the former today flat-surfaced and grey, the peak of the latter still hiding in mist. In such weather the road seemed longer, but at last they were approaching Torlinnhead, and there Geoffrey, after hesitation, turned off on a minor road that led to a village. Then there were other hesitant turns. They climbed a bleak glen, and turned again. Now a loch bounded the road upon one hand, and a ben that wasn't their ben soared on the other. Geoffrey pulled in and parked by the loch, leaving room for the Rover to park behind him. They got out.

'And this – this is that Rannoch?'

'Good lord, no!' Geoffrey grinned. 'But that's the Road to The Isles over there, and this fellow here has to be Schiehallion.'

'Schie . . .?'

'He turns up in a ballad. Ask George. He's bound to know it.'

'It would have to be weather like this,' Bridget complained. 'I've brought my camera, but what's the use?'

'Of course, I could do you a sketch,' Geoffrey smiled.

'You dare, Geoffrey – just you dare!'

But little by little the wrack was clearing from the sweeping view of the glen below, revealing a corner of Loch Tummel and a hint of the river flowing in from Loch Rannoch; while even the cindery peak of the ben was beginning to harden in the moist sky.

'It's a far country,' Geoffrey chuckled. 'And it's as well for us we brought the cars. If we were stuck with only a crummock we'd never make Rannoch in time for lunch.'

'What is that?' Gabrielle asked. 'A crummock?'

'I'm darned if I know myself,' Geoffrey said.

The road by Schiehallion was narrow and winding but fortunately they met no other traffic. It twisted its way through a series of grey hills where, later on, the heather promised to be spectacular. It ended in an easy run into the large village of Kinloch Rannoch, just beyond which opened an arresting prospect of the loch itself, thrusting westwards.

'This will be – what is it? The Road to The Isles?'

Quickly the few houses were left behind. For a while the loch-shore was fledged with trees, beneath which wood anemones bloomed luxuriantly. Then the trees began to fail, to be replaced by rough, boulder-strewn braes, and finally these too levelled out and the road proceeded across rugged open country.

Far ahead stood a range of jagged peaks, topped with snow more enduring than that of the night before; lower hills closed the prospect to the right, and spread in a vast amphitheatre around a far-distant boundary. Boulders were strewn over the plain they were traversing. They might well have been driving across a lunar landscape. The road rose, fell and made laboured detours to avoid areas of swamp, boulders and rocky outcrops. Did it go on for ever? That was certainly the impression, as mile followed painful mile, with the distant peaks seeming not an inch closer, or the country that unfolded one degree less hostile. But then, at long last, when all hope was fading:

'Look, my dear – a house!'

They had come to The Moor of Rannoch Hotel – with, behind it, and even less credible, railway lines . . . and a station!

The Jaguar paused as it came to the hotel, a discreet white-walled, slate-roofed establishment; then it drove on the few yards further to the elevated parking beside the station. Gently followed and parked beside it. Geoffrey was already out of the car.

'But this is fantastic – quite fantastic! Who would ever dream of catching a train here?'

He was staring down at the neat, granite-chip platforms, the smart, freshly painted buildings of a model wayside station. A loop-line encompassed it and there was a rusty siding across the tracks; a cottage, doubtless the station-master's, stood adjacent, and then there was the hotel. But nothing more.

'Perhaps they run it for the tourists,' Bridget said. 'There must be others who drive out here.'

'But to catch a train?'

'You never know.'

Geoffrey shook an unbelieving head. In fact, three other cars were parked there, but their occupants plainly were not waiting for a train. Some were taking photographs of the station and its name-plate, others strolling curiously along the platform.

'Do trains ever come here?'

Yes: the tracks said so.

'Well, it beats me,' Geoffrey said. 'Perhaps the local laird was a director of the company, and had his girl-friend installed at the hotel. But let's go down and take a look.'

Bridget fetched her camera from the car. Steps led down to the level of the platform, to reach which they must first cross the loop-line. The station was immaculate. Its granite chips were crisp, and the small flower-beds set among them tended with care. The waiting-rooms – there were two – were spotless and ornamented with vases of fresh-cut flowers. But the office was deserted, and they could find no timetable. It seemed like a station caught in a time-warp. The tracks departed, one way, into dividing braes, and the other across the moor to infinity.

On the far side of the station, through a gate, a path led to what appeared to be a derelict cottage, and then into the vast of the moor and its far-away hem of snow-clad peaks.

'Twelve miles of bog,' Geoffrey said. 'I looked it up. But there's a decent hotel on the other side. And that's Glencoe you can see over there. Anyone care to come for a stroll?'

Nobody did. Bridget took her photographs, and they climbed the steps again to the cars. Other visitors were making their way to the hotel, and it seemed a good idea to join them. But at the entrance, Bridget came to a halt.

'Look!'

She was pointing into the hotel-yard. Three cars were parked there. One was a Sierra; it was red, and sported an 'I support Rangers' sticker.

'It's the toy-boy's – I'd know it anywhere! And this must be where he's hiding out.'

'Hang on, Bridgie!' Geoffrey said hastily. 'He can't be the only Rangers supporter in Scotland.'

'But I remember the car, a red Ford – and this is just the sort of place where one would find him!'

'But the poor soul may be an innocent visitor –'

'No he isn't. You tell him, George. That's the car we saw parked at The Clachan.'

Gently said, 'Wait out here.' He went on into the hotel. Through a hall he came to a modest bar where visitors were already seated at the few small tables. None of them was Fowler. He approached the counter. A young girl who looked like a student was pulling a pint. She handed it to her customer, rang up the money, then turned a bright smile on Gently.

'You'll be wanting lunch, then?'

'First some information! Is the owner of the Ford in the yard a guest here?'

'The Ford? You mean the red one?'

'The Sierra with the Rangers sticker.'

'Oh aye!' the girl giggled. 'He's a bit of a laddie, that one. Do you know him, then?'

'Is he a guest here?'

'He is. But you won't be finding him around just now.'

'Then where will I find him?'

'I cannot just say. But he was planning to be back on the afternoon train.'

'The train . . .?'

'We do have them, you know! You can get through to Glasgow from here. But it was the other way he was going, through to Mallaig, and maybe Skye.'

Gently stared at her. 'May I see your book?'

'Robertson' was the name he found inscribed there. Fowler had checked in on the Monday evening, and they were holding his room for him till today.

'Where's your phone?'

'You'll find it in the hall.' The girl wasn't smiling at him now. 'There's nothing wrong, is there? He seemed a decent sort of fellow – just a roving eye, that's all.'

Gently rang Kinleary, and by luck was able to catch Blayne. He could almost see the puckering face of his colleague as he heard the information Gently was giving him.

'Mallaig, you say?'

'He probably spent the night there. He's expected back on the afternoon train. He's using the same name, Robertson, as he used at The Clachan, and may have used it when he booked in last night.'

'Aye, I'll be tellin' the lads up there. But like he'll be back on the train by now. You'll stay around Rannoch, man?'

'We'll stay around.'

'Fine,' Blayne said. 'Just fine.'

Gently hung up and went out to the others.

'Well?' Bridget demanded.

Gently nodded.

They had their lunch in the small bar, which by now was quite crowded. Its windows gave a view across the moor towards the south and of the line departing to far-away Glasgow. But Fowler would be coming from the other direction, provided he wasn't picked up on the way – at Fort William, for example, where Blayne would not have failed to warn the local police.

Could he possibly be unaware that he was being hunted? In the hotel he had chosen a likely hideout. It might well have been days before the police checked it out, and it might even have escaped their attention altogether. But then why, the next day, this excursion to Mallaig, with the increased risk of detection it involved? Mallaig was a port, but scarcely one that offered opportunities for an escaping fugitive . . .

While they ate, they were being watched covertly by the barmaid and by a man who appeared to be her boss. Something must have got round to the other guests too, since there was little conversation at the tables. Gently had inquired the time of the train: it was due, the girl told him, at two forty. Just now it was coming up to two, but before long there would be action enough around The Moor of Rannoch Hotel. He glanced down the road towards Kinloch Rannoch, but as yet no car had made its appearance.

'Are you expecting someone, then?' It was the man, who had come across to their table. 'I see you are looking, and Alison tells me you have been inquiring about one of our guests.'

Gently said, 'There'll be explanations later.'

The man stared at him with narrowed eyes. 'There will be no trouble, now?'

'We anticipate none.'

'Aye, as long as you hold to that,' the man said. 'Will I be getting you coffee?'

'Four coffees.'

'Four coffees.' He departed promptly.

'He wants to get rid of us,' Geoffrey murmured. 'I suppose there is no prospect of mayhem, George?'

Gently shook his head. 'Just a discreet arrest. As far as we know, Fowler isn't armed.'

'A simple tap on the shoulder.'

'Something like that.'

'Hush!' Bridget said. 'He's coming back with the coffees.'

'So, let us drink them quickly,' Gabrielle said. 'This man shall have no cause for complaint.'

But alas for good intentions: they had barely stirred the coffee when two cars arrived, and moments later a uniform man strode briskly into the bar.

'You have a Chief Superintendent Gently here?'

Distastefully, the landlord indicated Gently.

'Sergeant Brodie, sir, from Kinloch Rannoch! I've been told to make contact and to liaise with you.'

'Let's go outside!'

Brodie followed him out. The two cars were drawn up on the hotel apron. About them stood three other uniform men, while a fifth manned the radio in one of the cars.

'You have brought no plain-clothes men?'

'Ach no! We had no time to fetch one, in such a hurry. But the Chief Inspector is on his way here, and hopes to arrive before the train is due. You will be knowin' this Fowler by sight, he says, and you're fully informed about the affair.'

'There was no contact at Mallaig?'

'No contact. They just found the hotel where he spent the night. But by then the train was long gone, though he may have been cotched at Fort William. Drummond –' he addressed the man in the car – 'have we any word yet from Fort William?' The man shook his head. 'Aye well,' Brodie said. 'They would have to have been fly to nab him there.' He glanced into the yard. 'Would that be his car, sir?'

'The red Sierra.'

'Aye. I cannot think he will get to makin' a run for it. But you never know. So if your car is handy, sir – I'll be keepin' these two for other service.'

Gently fetched the Rover, and under the eyes of the hotel-keeper, parked it to block the red Sierra. By now the others had come out to watch, along with most of their fellow-lunchers.

'Just so,' Brodie said. 'Just so. And now we'd best be movin' into the station. And I'd soonest it was just us on the platform, unless some of these people are for catchin' the train.'

The police cars were moved up to the parking above the station and placed in positions that would expedite a clean get-away. One man was left with them to man the radio and one to guard the top of the steps. Gently, Brodie and the two others proceeded down to the station, where they were met by its anxious custodian: Brodie explained. The station-master, still anxious, elected to return to his office. Brodie eyed the long, track-encompassed platform.

'We'll need to be canny when we go to collect him. It'll be a man at each end, I'm thinkin', with you and me patrollin' the middle.'

'We could use extra men.'

'Aye. I just grabbed what I could and came runnin'. But the Chief Inspector will be bringin' more.' He glanced at his watch. 'Provided he gets here.'

'We could bring down the other two.'

Brodie thought about it. 'I don't just like leavin' those steps unguarded.'

'But the other?'

'Ach well! Why not? If there was news from up the line, we should have heard it before now.'

So the fourth man was fetched, and positions allotted, to the intrigued interest of watchers above, some of whom had brought their cameras and already were taking sighting shots. Brodie scowled up at them, but there was nothing to be done. He had no men to clear the parking. And just then a bell rang in the office, and the station-master signalled with a wide-spread hand.

'Five minutes to go – Chiefie's never going to get here!'

'Perhaps we should call the other man down.'

'But if those gawkers get here amongst us –'

'I think they have the sense to stay where they are.'

Brodie compromised. The man was called down, but only to the bottom of the steps. He had barely arrived when there was a stir up above, and someone shouted, 'It's coming – it's coming!'

'Steady, you lot!'

All eyes were turned up the track, to the hazy divide in the braes; and moments later they could see the blunt nose of the diesel locomotive heading towards them, smoke panting from its funnel. Its siren sounded. The station-master bobbed out. The speed of the train began to diminish. Then there was another stir above, followed by squealing brakes and the slamming of car doors.

'Stay with it – stay with it!'

The train was almost in. Gently turned to see Blayne tumbling down the steps. After him came Purdy and several uniform men, who at once spread out and came belting up the platform.

'We made it then – we made it!'

But only just. The train at that moment was gliding to a halt. Its handful of passengers had got to their feet and were staring in alarm at what was now a cordon of policemen.

'Where is he – where?'

Doors were yanked open, and passengers thrust aside by impatient constables. The guard had got down and was complaining loudly at this mass invasion of his train. Gently moved rapidly along the platform. Most of the compartments he passed were empty. Among the few passengers he caught no glimpse of the fair curly hair and boyish features of the fugitive. The last two coaches extended beyond the platform, but three of the men had already clambered into these. Had Fowler really been aboard that train? Might he not, at this very moment . . .

'Search the toilets – under the seats!'

The engine-driver had got down from his cab. The guard was arguing with the station-master, demanding that the train should be allowed to proceed. Then there came a cry from one of the spectators, who had climbed the fence at the highest point of the car-park. She was waving her camera wildly and shouting inarticulately.

'What does the fulish creature want?'

In a moment she was down from the fence and heading for the steps. A young woman with freckles and a pony-tail hair style, she dashed panting up to Blayne.

'Has the feller you're after frizzy fair hair?'

'Have you seen him, then?'

'Did you not hear me? He dropped off on the other side of the train, and now he's headin' into the moor!'

'Into the moor!'

'Aye, I was shoutin' – I saw him run across and leap over the gate.'

'Heaven presairve us!' Blayne was goggling, but he quickly pulled himself together. 'Get over there, some of you – get across there! If we lose him now we'll be needin' dogs and a helicopter.'

Men scrambled into the train to drop off on the other side

and go haring across to the gate. Brodie was summoning his men from the coaches, and the guard was swearing: 'I'll have to check every last one of those doors!' Blayne grabbed the young woman. He pleaded:

'You're sure now – you're sure? A youngish laddie with curly fair locks?'

'Yes, I'm sure! He was droppin' off the train almost before it came to a stop.'

Blayne groaned. 'He'll be away – he'll be away. And in a' those bogs and burns and lochans. If we do not get him the moor will – and likely one or two of us besides. Ach, the size of it!' He turned to Gently. 'But there cannot be much doubt now, I'm thinkin'. That's no honest chiel scamperin' off there – if we lay hands on him, we've got our man.'

Gently shrugged: it certainly seemed like it.

'But can I get away now?' the guard stormed. 'Man, we're ten minutes late already, and it will be as long again before I close those doors.'

'Ach, get on with it!' Blayne looked sick.

And now the audience above was beginning to filter down the steps. Brodie had gone across to organize the searchers. But no shout of any sightings was coming back across the tracks.

5

The train departed, leaving the station in the hands of the
excited sight seers. Gently got down from the platform and
crossed the tracks to join Blayne and Brodie on the other side.
Through the gate, the size of the problem was plain. An army
might have lost itself in that moor. The track petered out beyond
the empty cottage, which was the first thing the men searched,
and now they were spreading out, cautiously but unhopefully,
among the bogs, bracken and bushes on either hand. But . . . if
Fowler had kept going? By now he would have vanished in the
distant cover, stretching twelve miles to The Kingshouse Hotel
and to the road that unravelled Glencoe. Dogs, a helicopter
might find him, or he might vanish into the treacherous bogs;
but perhaps the most hopeful course would be to patrol the
boundaries and to leave the moor itself to drive him out. This
solution was apparently occurring to Blayne, as he watched with
impatience the motions of the searchers.

'Ach Purdy, we're gettin' nowhere. Better call the lads in.'

'We shall need the dogs, sir. And the chopper.'

'Well, we'll see about that. We'll see.'

'He cannot be that far.'

'Just call them in. Before one or other sets foot in a bog.'
Blayne looked up hopefully at the sky. 'It may just be that a
shower will be doin' the job for us.'

Gently returned across the tracks to find Gabrielle and the
others waiting on the platform. From the appearance of the sky
it seemed likely that Blayne's hopes would soon be justified.
Geoffrey gave Gently a hand up.

'No luck, then, for Dominie Sampson?'

Gently shrugged. 'If Fowler is out there, then it's he who will shortly be needing the luck.'

'I feel sorry for that man,' Gabrielle said. 'I do not think he is guilty at all. It is just that he sees all these policemen waiting, and thinks that his only chance is to run.'

'Ssh!' Geoffrey grinned. 'Or you'll make yourself unpopular with a lot of frustrated coppers.'

'Well, to me, he did not look like a murderer.'

'They never do,' Geoffrey said. 'At least, the amateurs.'

Bridget said tartly, '*If* they've finished with you, George, perhaps we can get back to the cars. It's going to rain again, and the sooner we make a start for home the better.'

In fact they got back to the cars only just in time, Gently after a last word with the moody Blayne. The rain swept down in sheets as they pulled away from the hotel. The moor seemed to retreat into the sullen downpour which was defying their threshing windscreen wipers, and it continued with little relief until they crossed the divide by Schiehallion.

'See if you can find the local station on the radio.'

After several attempts, Gabrielle located it. At 5 p.m. it delivered a news-flash about the affair at Rannoch Station. The search was still in progress. The conditions had delayed the use of a helicopter. Cars were patrolling the A82, and searchers with dogs had set out from The Kingshouse Hotel. But, as yet . . . Gabrielle listened with an intent, a pitying expression.

'Do you think that poor man can survive, in a place so very terrible?'

'He may have found shelter somewhere. Perhaps a shack erected there for walkers.'

'But if there is no shelter?'

'Then . . .'

They continued listening in for the rest of the journey. But by six, when they arrived back at Fern Cottage, there had been no more flashes about the affair at Rannoch Station.

'The rain has stopped, Bridgie. So we may as well take our constitutional.'

Over supper they had talked the matter out, though coming to no settled consensus of opinion. In Bridget's view, there could be no doubt: the flight of the fugitive confirmed his guilt. A quarrel must have developed on that fatal picnic and the lady was dead by the time her husband arrived there. Hadn't Fowler, from the start, behaved guiltily? It was he, not the doctor, who had fled the scene. And now, finding his arrest imminent, he had made this last desperate attempt to escape capture.

'I do not agree with that!'

The opposite viewpoint was Gabrielle's. For her, Fowler was simply a foolish young man, on whom the arrogant doctor was seeking to throw suspicion. For did he not have all the motives, ha? Was he not pretending innocence by going to the police? Oh yes! And on his evidence alone his wife is missing when he comes to the scene. It is the doctor who is guilty, ha-ha, and who the police this moment should be arresting.

Geoffrey's view was somewhere in between, though he too leaned a little towards the doctor: his account of the matter was certainly unsupported, and in the matter of motive there was no contest. At the same time . . . well, you couldn't overlook it! Fowler's behaviour had been distinctly questionable. If he, Geoffrey, had had to represent one of them, he would probably have had to toss up as to which it should be.

'And our cunning old maestro over there . . .?'

But Gently had ventured no opinion. It was then they noticed that the rain had stopped, and even that late sunshine was beginning to gild the ben. So they hustled through the washing-up, with Geoffrey, unusually, lending a hand, and set out for their customary stroll across the bridge to the welcoming Clachan.

The bar was crowded, and it was apparent at once that news of the day's events was common property. They found the landlord holding court amongst a cluster of regulars that included the garage-attendant and even the staid Collins. The landlord hailed their arrival with glee.

'And you were there, man – it's a' on the news! "A celebrated detective from Scotland Yard" – that's yourself, man. And you it was who spotted Fowler!'

'Have they caught him?'

'Na, but it cannot be long. They'll have the helicopter goin' by now. But you were there, man. You saw it a' happenin' – sit you down, man, and have a dram on the house.'

'Oh lord,' Geoffrey said. 'And we were hoping for a quiet drink!'

'Let's just get out,' Bridget said. 'Somehow, I feel like a stroll by the river.'

'We'd better have a quick one.'

'Then make it quick. And George, you sit down here at your peril.'

They collected their drinks, and to the landlord's dismay departed with them to the outside tables: deaf to his warning that the seats would be wet, and that there might be another shower before long. The seats were wet, so they crossed the road to lean on the wall that bounded the falls, now swollen impressively by the contribution of the rains.

'I don't want to talk about it,' Bridget said. 'And I don't want to hear other people talk about it. I just want to drink my drink and watch the jackdaws, and perhaps afterwards take a stroll.'

'This white stuff is sweet cicely,' Geoffrey said. 'Up here it takes the place of cow parsley.'

'And this bush with the flowers is *sureau*,' Gabrielle said. 'But I do not know what you call it in English.'

Gently merely lit his pipe and watched the smoke rising in the still, moist air.

Later, when they'd finished their drinks, they split up, Bridget and Geoffrey choosing to take their stroll upstream. Gabrielle, for her part, wished to visit the spot where the river flowed into the loch. So she and Gently crossed the bridge again and made their way down through the town.

'It is best this way, yes? Your sister will not want to pass by the police station. And you, my dear, I expect to be good, and to pass by on the other side of the street.'

Gently chuckled, and agreed. But it wasn't Blayne who interrupted their progress. Outside The Highland Arms, beside his car, the doctor stood staring at the evening sky. His eye fell on them. He watched them approach. Then suddenly he jerked down the steps to confront them. He said:

'You are an officer from Scotland Yard, I understand. And I wish to speak to you about this matter of my wife.'

* * *

He was flushed and very slightly trembling and his greyish eyes were set in a stare. He had planted himself firmly in front of Gently as though he had no intention of permitting him to escape.

'You have something to tell me?'

'We can't talk here! I must ask you to accompany me to my room. If your lady wife will kindly wait in the lounge, she will find magazines there, and I will order refreshment.'

Gently shook his head. 'Perhaps, in the morning . . .?'

'But it is essential that I speak to you now! Yesterday, I was unaware of your identity, or I would have requested an interview then.'

'You must know that my connection with the case is unofficial.'

'That is neither here nor there. I have observed your influence with Inspector Blayne, and it is to you I need to speak.'

'In that case – if you will make it brief.' Gently glanced at Gabrielle. Gabrielle gave an exaggerated imitation of his shrug.

'It shall be a glass of cold white wine!' she said.

They went into the hotel. The wine was ordered. Gabrielle was settled in the comfortable lounge. Then Angus led Gently up the sweep of stairs to a large room overlooking the street. It contained a miniature bar: Angus gestured to it, but Gently shook his head. Angus, however, poured himself a dram, and sipped it nervously before taking his seat.

'Now!' He set the glass down. 'The point of the matter is soon told. You have the culprit, or will arrest him shortly, and it is essential that I return to my practice in Bearsden.'

'You are asking me to intervene with Inspector Blayne?'

'To intervene – to talk sense to the man! There can be no reason to detain me any longer, and meanwhile my patients are suffering and my partner rushed off his feet. It is quite preposterous, and as a sensible man I ask you to recommend that I be allowed to return.'

Once more, slowly, Gently shook his head.

'But, for heaven's sake, man, you've got the killer!'

'Not yet.'

'But shortly you will have.'

'Shortly, it may be, the police will arrest Fowler.'

'But he's your man . . . are you saying he isn't?'

Gently said, 'We have yet to speak to him. At the moment, there are several questions to be answered. It may be that Fowler has those answers. We know only that he is a critical witness.'

'But –!' Angus's eyes were popping. 'Look here, we *know* he has to be the culprit. He was alone up there when I found him, and ever since his behaviour has been suspect. He ran. Why did he run? Why is he now evading arrest? And meanwhile I, who reported the matter, am cooped up here in what amounts to house-arrest. Is that fair?' He drank some whisky.

Gently said, slowly, 'But we shall need to ask him why.'

'Ask him –?'

'If he is the culprit, why he did it. Because his motives seem non-existent.'

'But I explained that!' Angus's glass was shaking.

'Perhaps not to the satisfaction of Inspector Blayne.'

'But – you heard me! It was the truth. If Maureen had been harassing him, anything could have happened.'

'That is your experience of her.'

'Yes!'

'She could provoke a man as far as murder.'

'As far as that – yes!'

'Any man.'

Angus pulled up short. 'What are you saying?'

Gently stared down at the street. 'Suppose there were other men. With other motives. Stronger motives. Wouldn't you say the police would be wise to treat the case with a degree of caution?'

Angus glared at him, breathing faster. 'And am I to accept that that is your opinion, too?'

'Let us say that I can appreciate Inspector Blayne's handling of the matter.'

'I see.' Angus swallowed whisky. 'Then I'm wasting my time in appealing to you. And it would be useless to provide testimony of Maureen's powers of provocation, since that would only be used against me.'

After a pause, Gently said, 'Was Fowler her first fling?'

Angus jerked his face away. 'Of course not.'

'You were aware of others?'

Finally, he nodded. 'But Fowler was the first one I caught her out with.'

'How would she manage it?'

'How? There's an invalid mother who lives in Edinburgh. That was her excuse, and she repeated it this time. Only this time I happened to have other information.'

'And this has been going on . . . how many years?'

The set of his mouth was savage. 'Does it matter? But I should have guessed sooner. She divorced another man to marry me.'

'You were her second husband?'

'Yes. Stephen Jamieson was her first.'

'Jamieson . . .?'

His mouth twisted further. 'The senior partner in the practice. Oh, I'm not proud of it. But it wasn't my fault. She divorced him after he went to jail – two and a half years in Barlinnie. He was struck off, of course. Then she married me.'

'What had Jamieson done?'

'Trafficked in drugs. I was obliged to give witness for the prosecution. It made quite a commotion at the time, but was excessively embarrassing to me. When he came out he tried to see Maureen and we had to get a court order to restrain him. It was touch and go for a time. But then he gave up and cleared out.'

'Have you seen him since?'

'Decidedly not. And I trust I never shall.'

'Or heard what happened to him?'

'No. If he'd had any sense he would have gone abroad.' Angus drank up his whisky. 'Any more snide questions?'

Gently continued to stare at the street. He said, 'If there were other boy-friends before Fowler, surely you would know about one or two of them?'

'And – if I did?'

'It might be useful to have their names.'

Angus slammed down his glass. 'I've had enough,' he said.

'I thought I would be talking to an intelligent man. But I find you are no better than your country colleague, so we may as well end this pointless exchange.' He paused. 'You still refuse to recommend my request to Inspector Blayne?'

Gently said, 'I think you have the answer to that.'

'In that case there is no more to be said. Please convey my apologies to your wife.'

He pointed to the door. He didn't get up. He kept his stare averted as Gently rose and left. Below, in the lounge, Gabrielle welcomed Gently with a sigh, and cast aside the copy of *The Lady* she'd been leafing through.

'Did he offer you a drink too, the good doctor?'

'Something like that,' Gently grimaced.

'My dear,' Gabrielle said. 'I cannot help it, but I do not very much like that man.'

It didn't rain again. They sauntered on through the cool calm of the evening. At the bottom of the street a junction led to the town's car-park, from which a path continued to the head of the loch. There the river, which was dashing down the falls, entered swiftly but smoothly the long reaches of pale water, passing by heathery rocks and a flat beach of grey shingle. Gabrielle chose a rock, and sat. Gently knocked out and refilled his pipe. The only sounds were of the murmur of water and the evening song of some bird.

'It is so peaceful here, yes?'

Above woods to their left rose the darkening ben. To their right, misty, forested braes stretched away into the gathering twilight.

'But for that poor young man – no peace! He is hunted and alone in a place so dreadful.'

'By now he may have been brought out.'

'Yes, to be accused of the death of that woman!'

'Blayne isn't a fool.'

'Ha, you say. But I am afraid. Afraid for that young man.'

Gently blew a ring. 'Let's just enjoy the evening. I think that bird out there could be a diver.'

So Gabrielle said no more, and they watched the evening

descend on the loch, the mist rising, the braes fading into silhouette, a single star riding over the ben.

Street-lights were sparkling in the town when they returned again up the street, and a light was showing in the doctor's window, above the grey Mercedes lurking below. Then, at the bridge, someone came running; it was the sleazy garage-attendant, Jock.

'Hang on – hang on! I've been sent to fetch ye. The chiel Hector is wantin' a word.'

'A word with me?'

'Aye. He had a phone call a while back.'

'Do you know what about?'

'I think I'm guessin' it'll be about the feller they're huntin' on the moor.'

'Oh no!' Gabrielle exclaimed. 'Oh no.'

'It canna well be about anythin' else.'

Gabrielle's hand tightened on Gently's arm. 'George, I think I'll go straight back to the cottage. You do not mind?'

Gently shook his head.

'Then I will see you soon. Please do not be late!'

She went. Gently followed the attendant across the bridge to The Clachan. He found the bar now almost empty and about to close for the night. The landlord, Menzies, was sitting at a table, with a half-empty glass before him; but he was on his feet in a moment when he saw Gently come through the door.

'Ach then, he found you – thank the lord! I was just wonderin' if I should not call Blayne.'

'You have heard news of Fowler?'

'News, he says! But let me clear the house and bolt the door.'

It was quickly done. Jock and the few hangers-on were thrust out. The bolts were slid on the formidable door, and Menzies beckoned Gently to the back of the bar.

'Listen – I'm in a tangle! I dinna ken quite how I stand with the law. But I'm to give you the message, he says, and I'm thinkin' you'll know what to do after that.'

'A message – from whom?'

'Why, who do you think? That laddie is not skulking around on any moor.'

'You're saying – Fowler?'

'Aye, who else? He was on the phone here just half an hour ago.'

For several long moments Gently stared at Menzies, then began to shake his head. 'That can't be so.'

'But I'm tellin' you it is! Half an hour gone by, he was on that phone.'

'It has to be a hoax.'

'No, man – no. Are you sayin' I don't know the laddie's voice? Was he not stayin' here over the weekend, and havin' a crack with me now and then?'

'He could never have got off the moor.'

'But the cunning chiel never was on it!'

'Not – on it?'

'Na, I'm tellin' you. He was back on the train when it pulled out. There's one of these bunkers, is there no', the manner of thing where they stow the ballast. And he's back through the fence and crouchin' behind it when all the polismen are out on the moor. Then he watches his chance and slips back aboard, just as the train is movin' out, and he tells a lady passenger who sees him that he's a plain-clothes dick under orders to stay with the train.'

'Then – where is he now?'

'Ach, would he be tellin' me? It's maybe Tyndrum or Crianlarich. But one thing's sure, he's no' on the moor, and like you should be dropping a hint of it to Blayne.'

Gently kept staring. Was it possible? Again he was seeing that scene at the station. And yes – such a bunker there had been beside the rusty rails of the siding. Bramble, bracken crowded close to it, while the ancient fencing offered small obstacle. And, when the train had slowly moved out, not an officer was remaining on this side of the gate. The driver's eyes would be ahead, the guard just ascending from the platform. With the one exception, the gaze of the passengers would be directed to the policemen on the moor. Yes . . . it fitted!

'And you say he left me a message?'

'Aye. For the polisman from Scotland Yard. And he's sayin' he

70

kent nothin' about this business till he heard of it on the radio this mornin'. Then he's a' of a tizzie, with the polis huntin' him and like to blame him for the job, and when he sees you a' lined up at Rannoch he just cannot bide to let you grab him.'

'But what's the message?'

'It's no' but this. The laddie is willin' to give himself up. But first he's for havin' a word with you, and I'm to tell you that he has information which could be useful.'

'Did he say what?'

'Na, no more than he tellt me from where he was ringin'!'

'Then how am I supposed to get in contact?'

'He'll be ringin' again, is what he said.'

'Ringing – you?'

Menzies nodded. 'And leavin' word where you can find him.'

'He knows I must arrest him?'

'Aye, he kens that. It's just he wants the chance of a word with you first.'

Gently shook his head. Blayne would have to be told this, and now there was a clue to where the net might best be spread. At the first or second stop down the line Fowler had doubtless left the train, and the odds were short that he would be picked up before ever he made his second call.

'May I use your phone?'

They had to wait half an hour before a car pulled up on the apron outside. Blayne looked tired. He listened to Menzie's account with narrowed eyes and a drooping mouth.

'And you're sure it's no hoax?'

'Na, na. I kent his voice as soon as I lifted the phone.'

'Ach, save us!' Blayne said. 'And all this time I've had men out on that bluidy moor. Lucky it is I've pulled them back now. There's just the road patrols and a car at Rannoch. If you're certain sure I'll lift them too, and put the ca' out Tyndrum way.'

The switch was made. Blayne sat himself wearily, and reached for the dram Menzies had placed at his elbow. He gave the landlord a meaning look, and Menzies discreetly withdrew himself from the bar. Blayne sighed, and drank. He looked at Gently.

'So what's your feelin' about the lad now?'

Gently shrugged. 'We'll need to talk to him first. But on the face of it, we may have to look further.'

'He could just be makin' out a case for himself.'

'That's possible.'

'Tryin' to use you, like, for his referee.'

Gently shrugged again.

'Ach well,' Blayne said. 'I'm glad to have the opinion of a man like yourself.' He took a slow sip from his glass. 'I've been gettin' information in,' he said. 'You would not have had words with the landlord at Rannoch, but he was tellin' me somethin' that made me think.' He drank some more. 'It's just this. Fowler booked that room on the Wednesday of last week. A double room. For himself and the lady. They were doubtless on their way there when they booked out from here.'

Gently said, 'And the same at Mallaig?'

'Just the same,' Blayne said. 'A double room for a Mr and Mrs Robertson. And furthermore, he'd booked their seats on the train.' He drank. 'So we're gettin' this picture,' he said. 'The laddie had planned out a tour for the two of them. And he is not hidin' up when he lights out for Rannoch, but just followin' the programme on his lonesome.'

'In fact it could be true . . . what he told Menzies.'

'I'm comin' to that opinion,' Blayne said. 'And I'm gettin' to be almighty curious about that information he says he has.'

'Information touching Angus.'

'Can there be any doubt, man?'

After a moment, Gently shook his head.

'It could be the clincher, you ken that. Just a glimpse of the lady comin' out of those bushes.'

'If that's what it is.'

'Ach, what else. And it will put the doctor right in our hands. I would not have you think I was prejudiced, but I've been itchin' to touch his shoulder from the start.'

Briefly, Gently recounted the interview that had taken place in The Highland Arms. Blayne listened with a glint in his eye, and ended by banging his glass on the counter.

'The nerve o'that man! The nerve of him! So I'm to be lettin' him slink off to Glasgow?'

'That was the gist of it.'

Blayne wagged his head. 'When I do, it will be between a pair of my officers. Ach, the nerve of him! Did you learn aught else?'

'Merely that the lady had been a divorcee.'

'That would not be news.'

'And that the lady's first husband had been Angus's partner, a Dr Stephen Jamieson.'

'Jamieson.' Blayne wrinkled his brow. 'Would that be the mannie who was sent down for trafficking some few years back?'

Gently nodded. 'He was struck off. His wife divorced him and married Angus. They had trouble with him when he came out. Angus had given testimony against him at the trial.'

'Man, the wickedness of the world!' Blayne said. 'But perhaps I might be havin' a wee word with Glasgow. And that was all?'

'Except there have been other lovers, who the doctor was reluctant to put names to.'

'Weel, weel,' Blayne said. 'Perhaps I would not just blame her, hitched up to a loon like yon fellow. And I'll be near to shaking Fowler by the hand if he can put me in the way of nailing the doctor.' He emptied his glass. 'But it's gettin' late,' he said. 'And I had best be hittin' the road. You'll be in touch if you get that message from the laddie?'

'I'll be in touch,' Gently promised.

Bridget and Geoffrey had retired by the time he arrived back at the cottage, and Gabrielle lay yawning on the settee, a radio talking softly beside her.

'You are late – and they have not caught him!'

He told her what had transpired at The Clachan. She listened sleepily, then giggled. She said:

'You know, I might use a young man like that!'

73

6

At breakfast Gabrielle had her radio tuned in to the local service, but still the only news was a rehash of the events of yesterday. There was one minor advance. The train Fowler had re-boarded had Glasgow as its destination, and the police there had been alerted in case the fugitive had remained on the train. But the alert would have come too late for Fowler to be intercepted at the station, and he might even have had time to visit his flat before a watch could be placed on it.

'So he could be anywhere,' Bridget said. 'He could simply have changed trains and carried on to London.'

'Or caught a steamer down the Clyde,' Geoffrey said. 'Or perhaps the next flight to New York.'

Bridget sniffed. 'This isn't a joke, Geoffrey.'

'Oh, I don't know,' Geoffrey said. 'It has its moments. I can't forget all those earnest policemen hunting for a laddie already long gone.'

'Just remember that he could be a murderer.'

Geoffrey shook his head. 'I would take his case tomorrow. Even if he did it I could swing it for him. The jury would be with him all the way.'

'But he didn't do it,' Gabrielle said. 'He wishes to talk to George, and to give himself up.'

'You see?' Geoffrey said. 'And that would be the verdict of any twelve good men and true.'

Bridget didn't look convinced. 'What is your opinion, George?'

'Oh, George doesn't have one!' Geoffrey said.

'George thinks with me,' Gabrielle said. 'The young man has been naughty, but that is all. Is it not so?'

'Until we can talk to him,' Gently smiled.

'That is to say, yes,' Gabrielle said firmly. 'And George at this moment should be at The Clachan, where it may be already a message awaits him.'

The rain had gone, but after yesterday's long haul nobody had much inclination to stir far. Bridget wanted to shop, Geoffrey to set up his easel, and Gabrielle was urgent that Gently should haunt The Clachan. The cottage had no phone. There could be no contact except by constant attendance at the hotel. It was not, perhaps, an appealing programme, but did he not owe it to the good Blayne?

'Most probably we shan't hear from him again.'

'Oh, my dear! Did he not promise?'

'By now, he may have changed his mind.'

'But no. It is on you that he is relying.'

However, at The Clachan they found no message, merely a voluble and inquisitive Menzies. Blayne had been on to him already, he told them, and now was down in the town. Had something turned up?

'He was inquiring after you, whether you had called in yet this mornin'. And if the laddie rings I'm to rush you word of it, and to give him a tinkle straight after. You would not have seen him now, the laddie?'

Gently shook his head.

'He was that keen to get a word with you.' Menzies' eyes puckered. 'Would you be for believin' him now, when he says he's innocent – with only the word o' yon doctor against him?'

Gently shrugged.

'Aye, I ken how it is.' But Menzies looked disappointed. 'Will I be pouring you a drink, now – a wee dram?'

'Not just now.'

'It's on the house, you ken.'

They went out into the sunshine again, to gaze at falls that were still in spate. Already the strollers were congregating, the outside tables beginning to fill. The tragedy had done no harm to The Clachan. Newcomers were pausing to stare, to converse in lowered voices. Then they would drift across, pause again, and finally filter into the bar.

'You – wish not to remain here?'

75

'There seems little point. If Fowler rings, it will go straight to Blayne.'

'But he will let you talk to him?'

'That's certain.'

'Then, perhaps we may join Bridget.'

They crossed the bridge; but had not got far when a patrol car drew in beside them. Blayne climbed out and, to his small surprise, Gently saw Angus seated in the back. He was staring straight ahead with the trace of a sneer on his podgy face. Blayne nodded towards him with a wink and drew Gently a little aside.

'So we've made a trifle o' progress the morn!'

'Progress?'

'We've identified the green car. It was seen by a couple who live in one of those houses where you turn off up the glen by the bridge. They had been away, you ken, for their son's wedding, and only got back last night, and one of the men here, who kent them, had the sense to go down there and have a word.'

'And they had seen such a car pass?'

'Both seen it and kent it – for why? It belongs to a near-neighbour, and at noon or thereabouts it went by heading up the glen.'

'They are sure of the identity?'

Blayne's head weaved. 'They're sure of the colour and the model! And it's a car they're often seein' around, so there is not overmuch doubt, I'm thinkin'.'

'And the driver?'

'They'll not swear to that. But they had small doubt at the time. And in case you should still be guessin', the name of the man who owns it is Collins.'

'Collins! But I thought you told me –'

Blayne's head bobbed again. 'And I'm fresh from havin' a word at the Motors with Neil Frazer and Scruffy Jock. They had the car in, no question, but the job was done before noon, and Scruffy Jock dropped the car off at the mill when he went to his lunch. He says he found the door closed, so he just put the keys through the box. And that's it. One green Volvo estate, all ready for a trip up the glen.'

'Have you spoken to Collins yet?'

76

'I'm about it now. And if the lady can spare you, I could wish to have you along.'

'And – Angus?'

'Just ballast.' Blayne winked at Gabrielle. 'I'm hopeful that the car may jog his memory. And – weel, he was reluctant to come along, and it pleased me fine to exert my authority!'

'You are a bad man, I think,' Gabrielle said. 'But I consent that George may go. But please do not be unkind to Mr Collins, who is my friend, and also a colleague.'

Gently got in the car beside the scornful Angus, and Gabrielle watched as they pulled away. They drove past the falls and into the cul-de-sac that ended at the grey stone mill. Its door was open. Two customers were emerging. And the Volvo estate stood parked in its slot.

'The car I saw was green, and this car is green. I cannot think what else you expect me to tell you. And since that concludes my part in the business, I assume that I am now free to leave.'

'Ach, not just yet, sir!' Blayne said. 'I'm wantin' you to have a good close look. It's maybe you saw more of the car than you're thinkin', so perhaps you'll just give it a few moments of your attention.'

Their driver had parked at a short distance, and now they were standing beside the Volvo. A 7-series with a recent date-letter, it offered few points for positive identification. There were no stickers, no dangling dolls, and the dusty paintwork was unmarked. At a glance, a car as anonymous as any Volvo well could be.

'Except for the colour, to me it suggests nothing.'

'But if you noticed the colour, sir, you noticed the car.'

'That it was green. And no more.'

'But if it was a car o' this heft, sir?'

Angus pouted at the car. 'That is possible.'

'It was no' a small car – no' a Mini?'

'Certainly not. It was of a larger description. Such a one as this is not wholly improbable.'

'And – comin' and goin' – you'll have given it a look, since each time you're tellin' us it's the same car – you could not have noticed that else?'

'Your logic', Angus said, 'would appear to be impeccable.'

'Then you'll be lookin' at the driver, maybe?'

'I may have looked at the driver.'

'And it was a man, like – no' a woman?'

'On the most fleeting of impressions, the driver was a man.'

'Fine,' Blayne said. 'Fine. And you'll be for describin' him?'

Angus said icily, 'He was not a woman.'

'But was he tall or short, man – young, old?'

'I regret I must let the matter rest at his sex.'

'Then you'd no' recognize him again?'

Angus didn't seem to feel it required an answer.

'He was not, for example, a man like yon?' Blayne pointed towards the door of the mill. Collins stood there. He was staring at Angus. And there was fear in the antique dealer's gaze.

'I – know that man!' Suddenly, the doctor's plump figure had stiffened. He glared towards the shrinking Collins, his fleshy hands working. 'Is he the owner of this car?'

'Aye,' Blayne said smoothly. 'He surely is.'

'Then it was he I saw on Monday?'

'You'll be tellin' me,' Blayne said. 'Is it comin' back now?'

'Ye-es,' Angus said. 'This is interesting. Very interesting indeed! His name for the moment escapes me, but I have certainly met this man before. How is he called?'

Blayne told him.

Angus's eyes glittered. 'Exactly so,' he said. 'Exactly so. Mr Dennis Collins. Formerly of Bearsden. And probably up the glen on Monday.'

'You are sayin' – ?'

But Angus ignored Blayne. He marched across to the antique dealer and planted himself before him. He stared into the man's frightened eyes. He said softly:

'So this is where you have hidden yourself – Mr Collins! Ten years ago you were thriving in Bearsden. Precisely why did you feel the need to remove yourself here?'

'I – I –' Collins stammered.

'When you were doing so well,' Angus murmured. 'Maureen alone must have paid your expenses – with her sudden enthusiasm for lustre porcelain. Her collection still occupies the parlour. No doubt you will recall that elaborate tea-set.'

'But it wasn't – what you think!' Collins exclaimed.

'It wasn't?' Angus said, his voice rising. 'All those expeditions to sales-rooms – with Edinburgh a principal venue? Did you think I was blind, Mr Dennis Collins? Did you think it was safe to carry on for ever? That Maureen would never grow tired of porcelain, and that Nemesis would never catch up with you? Well, you know better now, Mr Collins. And you dare to look me in the face? You have the effrontery to stand there and deny what even Maureen was obliged to confess?' He took a menacing step forward.

'Here, here – none o' that!' Blayne exclaimed. 'You've made your point, man, now stand back. You would not want me to put you inside for assault.'

'But this man was her lover!'

'I'm hearin' what you say.'

'And he it was who was up the glen!'

Blayne hesitated. 'You'll testify to that?'

Angus glared at him, his fists clenching.

'So you'll just calm down,' Blayne said. 'And leave the management o' things to us. And now you've had your say I'm thinkin' you'll do best to be shufflin' off back to The Highland.'

'But does it mean nothing that he was present in the glen?'

'That's for us to be decidin',' Blayne said.

'That man killed my wife!'

Blayne confronted him. 'Now – a word to the wise, Dr Robert Angus! One more such speech out o' turn from you, and you'll be inside before you can blink. That's fair warnin'. So now on your way – before I change my mind and put you where you belong.'

Angus eyed him savagely. 'I shall complain!'

Blayne pointed a finger towards the town. Angus went.

'Weel, weel,' Blayne said. 'One meets a' sorts.' He turned to the pallid-faced dealer in antiques. 'So now we can get to your business, Mr Collins. And for that, perhaps we'll be steppin' inside.'

'But that man – it was completely untrue!'

'I'm maybe thinkin' so,' Blayne said. 'But let's inside out of public view – our fiery doctor was pullin' in an audience.'

Shakily, Collins led them into the mill. Blayne left the driver stationed at the door. They went up the stairs to the main display area, then through a short passage to a private room. It was apparently both an office and a workshop and had a window that overlooked the falls. Collins stood by timidly while they entered, then dropped tremblingly on a chair. He faltered:

'It isn't true – any of it! I didn't move here for fear of him. And his wife . . . she was just a good customer. And I couldn't have *been* in the glen on Monday!'

Blayne glanced at Gently. 'All in good time! So where do you say you were on Monday?'

'Where? I was here, of course!' And Collins plunged his head in his hands.

'So you were here, then.' Blayne looked for a seat, but had to make do with a corner of a desk. A work-bench with tools was the only other option, and after hesitating, Gently hitched himself on it. The room had a sweet, pungent odour. An inlaid oval table stood by the bench. On the bench stood a bottle and some polishing materials, and it was from these that the odour appeared to emanate. Blayne observed the antique dealer with narrowed eyes. He said:

'Then there'll be just a wee truth in what the doctor was throwin' at you. You kent his wife back in the old days – it may be you kent her rather well.'

'But not like that!' Collins faced Blayne desperately. 'I knew her only as one of my best customers. She spent a great deal of money with me, and – well, we went to a few sales together.'

'A few sales.'

'It was quite innocent! We had to attend them on the view day. That meant staying overnight, of course, if it were somewhere distant, like Edinburgh.'

Blayne pursed his lips. 'And we're talkin' about the same lady – the one who was cuttin' a dash at The Clachan?'

'This was ten years ago!'

'Aye, it was. But I doubt if the lady has changed so much in the meanwhile.'

'It was just business, I tell you! She had a passion for lustre. It started with a jug I had displayed in my window. Then she showed me the catalogue of a sale at Motherwell, and wanted me to vet some pieces there and bid on them for her. It was simply business.'

Blayne's shaggy head swayed. 'If you're sayin' that's the manner of it,' he said. 'But it does not quite square with the lady's character, and I'm thinkin' she lost her taste for lustre a few years since, it may be ten. But you'd ken the lady when you saw her again?'

Collins gave Gently a fearful look. 'Yes.'

'And you did see her – that evenin' in The Clachan?'

Collins nodded, and hung his head.

'And she saw you?'

'No. I don't think so. I kept well away from her table. Once . . . well, I thought she gave me a look, but that was all. She wouldn't have wanted to recognize me.'

'But you saw her, you kent she was about. And maybe she was kennin' you.'

'I tell you, I kept out of her way!'

'Aye, I heard you,' Blayne said. He took a sighting shot at Gently. 'So we'll come to the mornin' after,' he said. 'The Monday morn. You would not have been across there havin' a coffee, say, before comin' back here to open up?'

'No, I wouldn't!'

'Just to glance at your paper, now?'

'I didn't go anywhere near The Clachan. I had my car to deliver at the garage, and that made me late opening the shop.'

'Your car to deliver,' Blayne said. 'Then we'll just carry on from there. A quiet mornin', was it, at the shop – no great rush of customers, I'm thinkin'.'

'What . . . do you mean?'

'Just tell me how it happened, man!'

Collins' drawn face flinched. 'It's always like that on a Monday morning – the visitors are still settling in. I had a

81

couple from Glasgow looking for amber and an American who bought a carriage clock. Then this gentleman's lady came in to look round. There was no one else before lunch.'

'So you did not mind closin' up,' Blayne said.

'I usually close the shop for lunch.'

'And a wee trip out – for a change of scene?'

'Sometimes. But I didn't do that on Monday.'

'You didna?'

'No, I didn't! I had my sandwiches in here. And I spent my lunch hour polishing a table – the twin of that standing there.'

Blayne stared at him with sharpened eyes. 'Tell me,' he said. 'You ken Geordie Robinson?'

'Yes, of course I do! He's a neighbour of mine, and he has also been a customer.'

'Aye,' Blayne said. 'So I understand. A man you ken and who kens you. And who's sayin' he was lookin' through his window around noon on Monday, and seein' a car he kens well drivin' up the glen.'

'He saw – me?'

'Is what he's sayin'.'

'But that's impossible! You must know –'

'Then,' Blayne said, 'there's the doctor, too. He's seein' such a car drive by when he's arguin' with Fowler. It does not stay, but turns in the loaning, and comes back past them down the glen. A car like yours. And the colour green. Which is why I had the chiel up here this mornin'.'

'But – if you asked at the garage!'

Blayne nodded. 'So I did. And they tellt me the car was back here by noon. And the laddie found your door bolted, that's true, so he just put the keys through the box.'

'Yes, but I didn't know. I was up here!'

Blayne's head wagged. 'And you expect me to swallow that?'

'But it's true. I didn't know the car was back till I came down to open, and found the keys.'

'Then what was the car doin' up the glen?'

'I tell you it wasn't me – and it wasn't my car.'

'Just one more green Volvo estate?'

'Yes! It's the only possible answer.'

82

'Ach!' Blayne shrugged his lean shoulders. He looked long at Collins, then at Gently. Gently said:

'We're not accusing you of anything, Mr Collins. Just seeking for vital information. You had a perfect right to drive up the glen, and you may well have seen something of the first importance.'

'But . . . I never did.'

'Would you know that spot?'

'Well – yes.' The answer came with reluctance. 'I may have driven up there once or twice, with my lunch. But I certainly wasn't there on Monday.'

'So you will know the layout.'

Collins nodded.

'You can recall the situation of the gorse. It closes in that part of the strath towards the loaning where people turn their cars.'

'Yes . . . I know it.'

'Then you'll appreciate this. Our information is that Mrs Angus had concealed herself there. From the strath she would be invisible, but not to the driver of a turning car. If such a driver did see her, his testimony is vital, and may very well clear up the case. If he did not, then we still need to know that, and it could lead to a similar conclusion.'

'And . . . it was . . . there?' Collins had paled.

'According to our information.'

'You mean . . .?'

Gently said nothing. Collins' faded blue eyes held tight to his for a painful moment. Then he buried his face in his hands again.

'Oh, poor Maureen! Poor, poor Maureen!'

'Did you see her?'

'Oh lord, I'd have given anything – anything!'

'But Collins, did you see her?'

'Anything at all!' He sobbed into his hands. Then he dashed the tears from his eyes and stared at Gently, his thin lips working. 'He did it, you know that – don't you? You've seen what he's like – violent! He'd beaten her before, she told me. And he'd have beaten her again if I hadn't cleared out. He struck me. I had to promise. And he – he was left alone up there with

Maureen! Why haven't you arrested him – why? What more can you possibly need to know?'

'I think you know that.'

'But don't you have enough?'

'I'll put the question to you again, Collins. Was it you who drove up the glen on Monday, and did you at any time catch sight of Mrs Angus?'

'I – if –' His mouth was trembling. His gaze wavered from Gently to the staring Blayne.

'Spit it out, man!' Blayne exclaimed. 'We'll no' eat you. Just the glimpse of her skirt is all we need.'

Collins was teetering, his mouth open. Finally he gave a wrenching groan.

'No. No. I can't do it!'

'Ach, come away!' Blayne said.

'It's no use. I wasn't up there.'

'Man, you were seen. Geordie Robinson saw you.'

'No. It was someone else.'

'But your car was here – ready to hand.'

'It wasn't my car. It wasn't me. I was here in this room. I'm sorry.'

'Ach!' Blayne exclaimed in disgust. 'We're tellin' you, man, this is vital. If you want that doctor to get his deserts, you'll just come clean about Monday.'

But Collins was shaking his head, tight-lipped.

Gently said, 'Then that is your answer?'

'Yes . . . it's the truth.'

'And it had better be!' Blayne snarled. 'Or we'll be havin' you in too as an accomplice.'

'Perhaps', Gently said, 'you would like time to think it over?'

But Collins merely went on shaking his head.

'The mean-spirited loon. He could have sewn this up for us!'

They were back outside in the car. Blayne was staring with a malevolent eye at the dusty Volvo standing in its slot. Collins had accompanied them to the door, but not another word had he spoken. Silently, he had wedged the door open again before departing up the stairs.

'He was out there, I'll have five pund on it, but he's decided that he's stayin' clear. Or maybe he's scairt of what the doctor may do to him if he learns that the loon has been squealing. Would you not say so?'

Gently shrugged. 'He may have been out there, and still not seen the lady.'

'But that will be castin' us back on Fowler, and I was thinkin' we were giving him a bill o' health.'

'Perhaps not entirely.'

Blayne stared.

'That phone call may just have been a blind,' Gently said. 'It could have been intended to take the heat off Fowler, to make it easier for him to slip away.'

'Ach, surely not!'

'It's possible.'

Blayne thought about it, then shook his head. 'Puttin' it all together, and matchin' him with the doctor, I'll keep my money where it is. He had no reason for it, him. I'd sooner back yon loon in there. He could have slipped over and attended to the lady while the doctor and Fowler were goin' hammer and tongs.'

Now it was Gently's turn to shake his head. 'I think perhaps we should put Collins on hold. He may have been there, but I think we have to assume he saw no sign of Mrs Angus.'

'But then we're stuck with Fowler.'

'Not necessarily. She may have been too well hidden in the bushes. We can only hope that Fowler means to come across, and that he has testimony that will settle the matter.'

Blayne sucked in lank cheeks. 'He's bottom o' the league in my reckoning,' he said. 'And the doctor, he's leading the division. And I'll be pencillin' in Collins somewhere between. He just could have done it. He was there. It has to lie somewhere between those three. The doctor says Collins, and Collins says the doctor, and the Fowler laddie we've yet to hear from. Would you say that was fair?'

'As long as Collins stays in pencil. He may still have told the truth about his movements.'

Blayne hesitated. 'You mean, there may be someone else?'

'With such a lady,' Gently said, 'It has to be considered.'

Blayne thought about it. He frowned.

'Have you talked to Glasgow?' Gently said.

'Aye, I talked to them.'

'And?'

'They are still rememberin' the bother with the doctor's partner. But that was twelve years since, and they have not seen him for almost as long – they were half-wonderin' if our man might not have had a hand in that, too. But comin' a bit more up to date, they're tippin' me a laddie called Gordon. He's an architect livin' at Milngavie, and he was the lady's latest but one.'

'And he was loose on Monday?'

'Aye. He was casin' a job over at Dunkeld. And here's the pith o' it – he was drivin' a green Volvo, though it may not have been an estate.'

'And he would have passed by here?'

'Like as not.'

'And your witness may have mistaken the car?'

Blayne sighed. 'That's just a possibility, though not one I'm hangin' too much hope on. Ach, no – I'll be followin' it up, but to my mind the right car is standin' just there. And now I'm thinkin' it's time to check with The Clachan, if only to put an honest thirst to rest.'

They drove back slowly across the narrow, busy bridge, and found parking with difficulty on the other side. But as yet there was no message from Fowler: a draught of cold bitter was their only reward.

7

'If the Perthshire Constabulary can spare you, George, we were planning a drive over to Strathtudlem. It may have altered since we were there last time, but I feel we ought to pay it a visit.'

They were lunching on fresh salmon steaks which Bridget had procured from a visiting fishmonger, who had also supplied her with fennel; the result had won praise even from Gabrielle.

'It's only a few miles, and I would like to visit the wool shop. Then we can have coffee at The Bonnie Strathtudlem, and perhaps take in the Skilling road on the way back. Does that suit people?'

'I wouldn't know,' Geoffrey smiled. 'But it will certainly bring back a few memories.'

'Ha, the ramping hizzie!' Gabrielle said. 'But I do not care, she shall not frighten me.'

'Oh, what nonsense!' Bridget said. 'Stop teasing people, Geoffrey. Is it all right, George?'

Gently nodded. 'I think I may safely leave matters to Blayne.'

So, when the tidying-up was done, Jaguar and Rover set off for the road heading south, passing by the mill, which appeared to be deserted, and by The Clachan, where every table was occupied. Gabrielle had given the mill a searching stare. Then she shot a quick little look at Gently.

'It is true, you think? He was the lady's lover?'

Gently slowed to avoid some pedestrians. 'Probably.'

'You do not know for certain?'

'From his behaviour, more likely than not.'

'Ah!' Gabrielle sighed. 'I am thinking so too. He is not all gem-stones and furniture, that man. Underneath, he is also

87

a romantic. I am understanding why the lady had a fling with him.'

Gently smiled. 'I will take your word for it!'

'But – it was he who was up the glen?'

'I'm rather afraid so.'

'Afraid?'

Gently changed up to speed after the Jaguar. 'It would make him the third man on the spot. The third with connections with the lady. It is a point that hasn't escaped Blayne.'

'You – cannot mean?'

Gently nodded. 'He would have had a possible opportunity. The gorse would have hidden what was happening from the others. And they were taken up with the row between themselves.'

'But why would he do . . . that?'

'He may have nursed a grudge. It was because of her he had had to leave Bearsden.'

'And so he would – strangle her?'

'On the impulse of the moment. And then dispose of the body in the river.'

Gabrielle stared ahead at the Jaguar. 'No,' she said. 'I do not believe this. Of some other man, yes, perhaps, but not of the man who is selling me this brooch.'

'That must free him from suspicion?' Gently smiled.

'Do not laugh at me, George Gently! I am talking to this man, I am studying his character, and he is not such a one as would strangle a lady. He is gentle, he is a romantic, he had once a wife who he loved. I am trusting him, except in business. It takes a woman to know such men, yes?'

'Perhaps I should be jealous,' Gently smiled.

'Still you are laughing at me, George! But you would do well to listen to your Gabrielle, who all her life has dealt with such people.' Gabrielle gave her head a toss. 'And it is I, I who should be jealous. Are we not going to this village where you stayed with your Brenda, not to mention the ramping hizzie?'

'That was before I met you.'

'I do not care. I have a right to be jealous. And I will not forgive you, nor the good Blayne either, if you go on suspecting my poor colleague. This is understood?'

88

'Understood,' Gently smiled.

'So. Now I shall devote myself to admiring the scenery.'

By now they had reached the main road and were climbing the spectacular pass through Glen Donach where, on the opposite braes, an abandoned railway line pursued its airy course. Then they swept down past Loch Cray and the junction of the back road to Skilling, and shortly were cruising into the long, level street of Strathtudlem village. Beside the street, since their earlier stay there, the Forestry had added a pleasant picnic-park. Into this Geoffrey turned, Gently followed, and the two cars parked in the shade of birches. Gabrielle loosened her belt.

'You', she said, 'were not serious, were you?'

'Not very,' Gently said. 'But now let's forget it.'

'Aha. And I will concentrate on being jealous.'

'First,' Bridget greeted them, 'I want to visit the wool shop. Then we can stroll a bit before we go for coffee.'

As it happened, Bridget got stuck in the wool shop, where the proprietress was an expert in the mysteries of Fair Isle, and it was not until the time for coffee that the party joined up again. Geoffrey wanted to visit an exhibition being offered by the Forestry; Gabrielle to stand on the bridge where the river formed a torrent. Then, it was inevitable, she crossed over to the back road, where a finger-post pointed out the track up the braes. She stared at it solemnly. Then at Gently.

'This . . . is how it was before?'

'More or less.'

'And up there you went?'

'A long time ago. When you would still have been Madame Hénault.'

'I do not wish to be reminded of that!'

'As I said, a long time ago.'

Gabrielle feinted a slap, but then took his arm and they strolled on beside the river, though from time to time, where the trees permitted it, she would glance up at the peak that lifted above them. They got back to find Bridget just emerging from the wool shop, followed by a Geoffrey laden with plump packages. Fortunately the hotel was just across the road, and they had no difficulty in commandeering a table.

'Four coffees – and some of those pastries.'

The waitress hesitated, staring at Gently. Then she pencilled the order on her pad, and stared at him again before departing.

'She remembers us,' Geoffrey said. 'I'll think of her name in a minute. Can you remember, Bridgie?'

'It was Mattie,' Bridget said. 'And she was rude on that occasion, too.'

'Didn't Blayne rather fancy her?'

'He was drunk that evening.'

'You could be right,' Geoffrey grinned.

But it was a man who brought their tray to them and, with a flourish, laid out the cups and plates. Then he stood by, holding the tray, a curious glint in his eye.

'You wanted something?' Bridget said.

'Ach no, not exactly that!' the man said hastily. 'But Mattie was sayin' – if it's no' impolite – is not this gentleman the detective from London?'

'And if he is?'

'Ach, nothing at all! Just that I'm wishin' him well with the doctor. Because there was a time before, you ken – but doubtless he will have heard a' that from Inspector Blayne.'

Gently selected a wicked-looking fruit slice. 'Would you be acquainted with Dr Angus?' he asked.

'Not exactly acquainted, you ken. But I was barman at The Brig when it was a' goin' on.'

'The Brig?'

'The Brig-o'-Doon. It's gae handy for couples up from Glasgow. And it was there the doctor brought the lady – but the name he put in the book was no' Angus.'

'Dear me!' Geoffrey said. 'The naughty doctor!'

Gently said, 'We are talking of the late Mrs Angus?'

'Aye, who else? But she was not Mrs Angus then. And that's the whole matter, as some of us saw it.'

'The whole matter . . .?'

'Was it not after that when the lady's husband was put in jail? And who was it dropped a word to the polis, and stood up in court and swore he was guilty? Aye –' the man nodded his head – ' and some of us thought there was a deal more to it. They was thinkin' it was Angus who should have stood in the dock, and no' the poor fellow Jamieson, his partner.'

'I love it!' Geoffrey said. 'Do tell us some more.'

'I think it's just scandal,' Bridget said.

Gently tackled the fruit slice. Through a mouthful, he said, 'And this is all of "the time before" you mentioned?'

'No, it is not.' The man jiffled with the tray. 'And but for what's happened I would not be speakin' it. But it's been on my mind since the moment I heard, and maybe on the mind of other folk, too.'

'So what was that?'

'It was the body in the Clyde.'

'The body – ?'

'Aye.' The man's head kept nodding. 'It was too far gone, and some chiel had stripped it, but the rumour was it belonged to Jamieson.'

'Just a rumour.'

'Man, a strong rumour. It was just after Jamieson came out of jug. He was after claimin' his property, that was well-kenned, and like to start a law suit against the lady.' The man stared hard. 'He was out at The Brig. He was lookin' for evidence that they had stayed there. He was for pullin' me in to give testimony, but you ken the boss was no' eager that I should.'

'Gosh,' Geoffrey said. 'And then they found the body?'

'It was not so very long after that.'

'And they couldn't identify it? Teeth, that sort of thing?'

'Geoffrey, please!' Bridget said.

The man looked askance at Geoffrey. 'Then perhaps you'll be tellin' me this,' he said. 'Whyfore was Jamieson never seen after that – nor ever again, after all these years?'

'Perhaps he went abroad.'

'Aye, you may say so. But other folk have other ideas. And now it's a' happenin' over again – and this time no doubt about whose body.'

'Both times the doctor?'

'It worked for him before.'

'I think it's all nonsense,' Bridget said. 'And now, I would

91

like to drink my coffee in peace, with no further discussion of putrefying bodies.'

The man hesitated, looking keenly at Gently. He said, 'And you'll be for arrestin' him – you've settled on the doctor?'

Gently ate another mouthful of slice. He said, 'If I may have your name, I will pass it on to Inspector Blayne.'

'My name! But he'll no' be needin' that.'

'Inspector Blayne may require your statement.'

'Ach no – a' this is well-kenned – I'm amazed you have not heard tell of it yourself!'

'Still . . . your name?'

It was Hamish McAndrew, the present manager of The Bonnie Strathtudlem. He gave it with all reluctance, and departed promptly, carrying the tray.

'You surely shut him up, George!' Geoffrey chuckled. 'But do you think there can be anything in what he says? I must say I rather like the idea of our doctor being a duplicate killer.'

'Be quiet, and eat your pastry,' Bridget said. 'I thought that here, if anywhere, we'd get a rest from this business. But no. Wherever George shows his face there's some crackpot, ready to pounce on him.'

'But Bridgie, it's a whole new angle!'

'It's stupid gossip,' Bridget said. 'George doesn't believe it, or this minute he'd be on the phone to his beloved Blayne.'

'Of that doctor,' Gabrielle said, 'I could believe it. But this is what you call hearsay, yes?'

'And that's often the best part of the evidence,' Geoffrey grinned. 'How dull our courts would be without it!'

'Geoffrey,' Bridget said.

Geoffrey grabbed a pastry. For a while, there was silence at the table. Behind the counter at the back they could see Mattie and the manager in subdued conversation, with their faces turned towards them.

They returned as planned, by the back road, which ravelled its narrow way between strath and braeside, with views ahead of the Braes of Skilling, and finally of the thrusting reaches of the loch. Gently pointed out the knoll from which the ramping hizzie had cast her scorn at the 'English craturs', and below which, on his illicit occasions, the Laird of Knockie had concealed his car. Gabrielle observed the feature sternly.

'It was from there you went with her up the mountain?'

'Not then. I hadn't got to know her.'

'But later you did?'

'It became essential.'

'Ha,' Gabrielle said. 'This you tell me. First with your Brenda, and then with the hizzie. It is perhaps something in the air up here.'

'That was Brenda's theory,' Gently said.

'Remind me', Gabrielle said, 'to hit you, when you are not driving a car.'

At The Clachan they paused briefly, but still there had been no message from Fowler. Blayne had called for a dram, Menzies told them, but if there were news he had not divulged it. Business was still booming, the bar, the outside tables crowded. Gently glanced round to see if Collins were present, but of the antique dealer there was no sign.

'Tonight, we go somewhere else for our drink, yes?'

Gently shrugged. He had almost given up hope of a contact with Fowler. Either the young man had changed his mind in the interval, or the police were making it difficult for him to get to a phone.

'I can call back again last thing.'

'We can, perhaps, try that hotel by the lake. There it will be quieter, I think, and the good landlord will not annoy Bridget.'

But Bridget had had enough of hotels, and she had also her purchase of wool to absorb her, while Geoffrey was content, as usual, to settle down with a pad and pencils. So, after the evening meal, they set off on their own to the hotel at the other end of the town, along the street grown now so familiar, past the garage, The Highland Arms, the little group of shops. The grey Mercedes had never budged, but tonight no doctor stood taking the air. At the garage Scruffy Jock gave them a wave, and outside the police station stood a solitary patrol car. Gabrielle gestured towards it.

93

'You do not wish to report? About the body that was taken from the Clyde?'

'I think it will keep!'

'You are not believing, ha?'

'I think probably Blayne is advised of it already.'

Gabrielle sighed. 'There is so much mystery! All the time we are hearing new things. I am wondering, now, if it will ever be known how that poor lady met her fate.'

'There are still lines of inquiry to be followed up.'

'Is all the same, if they have nowhere to go.'

'So, let's have our drink. And enjoy the evening.'

Gabrielle sighed again. 'Perhaps that is best.'

They crossed the bridge where the Eden river flowed softly below to meet the loch. The hotel, which took its name from the bridge, was certainly quieter than the popular Clachan. Only two of its outside tables were occupied. At one sat a bearded gentleman, alone. He looked up as they approached, then stared intently as they went by him. They bought their drinks, and selected a table. It gave a view across the loch to the folding braes. The last sun was still brightening their tops, and mist was delicately rising from the waters below. They sipped their drinks.

'You'll forgive me, now, but wouldn't you be Mr and Mrs Gently?'

Well, it probably had to happen! The bearded man had approached their table.

'I'm Tosh McDermid, at your service! I've just got back from Auld Reekie. I met a friend of yours there, Andy Reymerston, and he told me you were staying in Kinleary.'

'Andy . . .?'

'He's exhibiting there – we're both painters, you understand. He gave me permission to make myself known to you, so be it our paths should cross. And then I get back here and learn of this business that went on up the glen, and that you were giving the local Inspector a hand, and – well, I'm most happy to make your acquaintance!'

He thrust out a firm hand which, after a moment's hesitation, Gently accepted. Then he bowed to Gabrielle, who acknowledged him with a small inclination of her head. A man in his

94

forties, with a mop of chestnut hair to go with a full beard, clad in jeans, sandals and a jazzy sports-shirt. He'd brought his glass along with him.

'You had better sit down, Mr McDermid.'

McDermid drew up a chair without a second invitation. He took a preliminary swig from his glass, then fixed Gently with an eager brown eye.

'I'm going to ask you, of course – you don't mind? – but have you caught the fellow yet? I mean living where I do, in the glen, it happened almost at my front door.'

'You live in the cottage up there?'

'Absolutely. And I must have been there when it happened. I was packing stuff for the exhibition till three, and I understand it was all over by then. So . . . have you got him?'

'The inquiry is proceeding.'

'But surely – I mean! There's only one man in it. The boy-friend you just have to rule out, and that only leaves the obvious person.'

'That is being given due consideration.'

'You're saying – it wasn't him?'

Gently shrugged.

'You are being too naïve, my friend,' Gabrielle said. 'It is not in this way that policemen work.'

McDermid looked puzzled. 'Perhaps I am naïve,' he said. 'But that's how it sounded from the way it was told me. Coming in, I had a pint at The Clachan, and that's where I first heard the news.'

'And perhaps that explains it.'

McDermid shook his head and applied himself to his glass.

Gently said, 'You were at your cottage till three on Monday?'

'Yes. Packing up for the exhibition.'

'In your studio?'

'Yes, of course. I even grabbed my lunch in there.' He paused. 'Are you suggesting I could have seen something?'

'There can't be so many cars using the glen.'

'No, you're right. And I did see . . .' He frowned at his glass. 'Let me think!'

'Between noon and one is the critical time.'

'Yes, I know! I'm trying to remember. I think I saw a

couple go by. And then there was old Dennis. But he didn't stay long.'

'Dennis . . .?'

'The fellow at the mill. He sells a picture of mine now and then. He lives in the house just round the corner here, and sometimes takes his lunch up the glen.'

'And . . . on Monday?'

McDermid stared at Gently. 'Oh my God! Do you think he ran into them?'

'You said he didn't stay long.'

'No, he didn't. He must just have driven down there and come straight back again. Oh lord – poor old Dennis!'

'He followed the other two cars?'

McDermid nodded. 'There was a red one . . . it had a couple in it.' He closed his eyes. 'That would have been the woman?'

'A red Sierra.'

'I didn't notice. It went by the cottage before the others. Eleven thirty perhaps, or earlier. But I did notice the woman. She had long black hair.' His head sank. 'My God, I feel ill! It could only have been . . . how long? . . . before.'

'Another car followed it.'

'I don't want to remember!'

'It might be helpful if you would.'

He closed his eyes tight. 'It would have been him. That murdering sod. And I never guessed . . .'

'But you did see the car.'

'All right! It went by about half an hour later. And all I noticed was that it was large and had only the driver in it.'

'Would you remember the colour?'

'Grey. It gave the impression of being expensive.'

'But did you notice the driver?'

'No. Except that he seemed to be dressed in a suit.' McDermid grabbed his glass and drank. He sat staring at nothing, his mouth tight. Gently said:

'And then you saw your friend.'

'Yes. Dennis.'

'You can be quite certain of that?'

McDermid shrugged impatiently. 'Do you think I wouldn't know his old tank? I saw him going and saw him coming. It

96

couldn't have been more than twenty minutes. He must have seen what was going on there and decided he didn't want any part of it. Haven't you talked to him yet?'

'We have talked to him.'

'Then you must know all about it.'

'But, Monsieur McDermid!' Gabrielle exclaimed. 'Your poor friend is saying that he was never up there.'

McDermid stared at her. 'He's saying that?'

'But yes. On Monday, he says, he never left his shop.'

'But – I saw his car. I'm positive.'

'Oh monsieur, there are many other such cars!'

'A Volvo. A green estate.'

'And can there be only one like it in Scotland?'

McDermid stroked his beard. 'Well, I thought it was him! Just old Dennis going past up the glen. But if he says it wasn't, then that's that. It would have to be another car like his.'

Gently said, 'You didn't recognize the driver?'

McDermid shook his head. 'I didn't particularly look. I glanced up and saw the car, and took who was driving it for granted.'

'This could be important.'

'Sorry and all that. I did happen to be busy at the time.' He drank. 'I saw the red car come back. That was only a short while after the Volvo. Then –' he drank again –' the other car. And that was much later.'

'Can you give me an estimate?'

'Nearly three. So he'd have been up there two hours on his own. Good enough?'

Gently stared at him. 'It confirms information we already have.'

'So,' McDermid said, 'what's holding you up? Or am I still being too naïve?'

'Much too naïve, monsieur,' Gabrielle said. 'Perhaps our good friend Andy should have given you a warning.'

The painter lingered on for another round, then sought his car and departed. The sun had long vanished from the braes and lights were glittering towards the town. A little chill was in the air. The mist that clung to the loch had grown denser. Gabrielle had paid a brief visit in the hotel, and when she returned Gently knocked out his pipe.

'Time to go, yes?'

'First, just a small errand.'

'Ha, you too?'

Gently shook his head. 'A small errand at the house round the corner. In case a certain person may be wishing to change his mind.'

'But – it is getting late.'

'This could be vital. If you wish, you may wait here at the hotel.'

Gabrielle stared. 'Then this I will do. And please do not be so very long, George Gently.'

She went back into the hotel and Gently crossed the bridge to the beginning of the glen road. No difficulty arose in identifying the house: the green Volvo estate stood parked in its drive. Shrubberies surrounded it. Across the road, it looked out over unfenced bushy strath. A light showed in one of the downstair windows; Gently advanced to the door and pressed the bell. After some moments, he heard the unmistakable sound of a guard-chain being applied to the door. Then it gapped open.

'You!'

'Just a word, Mr Collins.'

The antique dealer stood staring with frightened eyes, his breathing fast, his mouth dropping.

'Is it . . . have you come here . . .?'

'If I may come in for five minutes?'

'But why – what's it about?'

'We can talk about that inside.'

For a moment it looked as though he might slam the door, then, with a trembling hand, he removed the chain. He led Gently into a room stuffed with furniture, pictures and shelves of china.

'Now – please!'

Gently cleared a chair of some leather-bound books, and sat. He said:

'You'll have had time to think matters over, Mr Collins, and

I'm wondering if you can't see your way to being a little more helpful.'

'But I can't – I've told you everything.'

'We won't blame you for . . . elaborating . . . your statement.'

'But . . . how? You know everything. There's just nothing more to tell.'

'Nothing more?'

'No – nothing!'

Gently looked at him, and shook his head. He said, 'This evening I was talking to a friend of yours. He had just got back from Edinburgh. He had been setting up an exhibition of his pictures there. Tosh McDermid. Who lives up the glen.'

'Tosh – yes. But what . . .?'

'He was in his studio on Monday, packing pictures for the exhibition. He saw three cars go by – Fowler's, Angus's. And yours.'

'Mine! But how could he?'

'He said the car was familiar to him and that he'd seen you drive by on previous occasions. On this one you returned rather promptly, as though you had merely turned round and come back again. You were followed soon after by Fowler and, after a longer interval, by Angus.'

'But this is impossible!'

'Are you sure of that, Collins?'

Collins also cleared a chair, and sank on it. 'This is a nightmare!' he exclaimed. 'Tosh couldn't have seen me. I tell you again – I was never there.'

'McDermid seemed very certain.'

'But you've got to believe me!'

'Your car was available at that time.'

'Only I didn't know that!'

'And Collins, I don't have to remind you how critical your testimony could be in this matter.'

He hugged himself, groaning.

'Well?' Gently said.

'I . . . can't. I wasn't there!'

Gently said, 'If you are lying, it could mean trouble for you.'

'It's no good. No good. I can't!'

'We won't blame you, if you tell us now.'

He gave a wrenching groan. 'But I can't . . .'

'Very well, Mr Collins.' Gently got to his feet. Collins stared up at him, the terror back in his eyes.

'You aren't going to –?'

Gently shook his head.

'But – ?'

'Just now, I will merely wish you good-night.'

He let himself out. As he passed the Volvo, he reached out mechanically to feel the bonnet. It wasn't quite cold. He fetched Gabrielle. At The Clachan, there still was no message from Fowler.

8

'You think my poor Collins did see the lady, but that he is too afraid of the doctor to tell you.'

It was another brilliant morning, with the distant ben sharp in the early sun. From their window, using glasses, it was just possible to distinguish climbers as they wrestled with the final drag to the summit, their triumph sometimes signalled by waving arms before exhausted bodies collapsed prone on the rocks. But that came later. At this hour of the day the majestic peak stood deserted, every line, cleft and detail picked out by the cool sunlight. The roofs of the town below were still largely in shadow, while the cars in the forecourt remained misted with dew.

'You can see his point,' Geoffrey said. 'He would be asking for trouble if he admitted it. It would simply be his word against the doctor's, and that might really drop him in it.'

'But who shall be taking the doctor's word, ha, when he has the reason and poor Collins has none?'

'It's a good line for the defence,' Geoffrey said. 'But it needn't stop them looking hard at Collins. They might think he bore a grudge against the lady. She was the cause of his having to clear out of Bearsden. So there was opportunity, and he took it. There's a sound case for the prosecution in that.'

'Yes, but this doctor is already killing once!' Gabrielle objected. 'You shall not forget the body in the Clyde.'

'That's just the text according to McAndrew.'

'Yes, and twice he is putting the body in the river!'

Geoffrey shook his head. 'All good defence stuff! But I

don't think it would bother the prosecution, just make a few headlines in the Sunday papers.'

'But we have met this doctor, and you have not.'

'Point conceded,' Geoffrey grinned. 'I probably wouldn't like his face either.'

'And so?'

'I think I'll settle for another piece of toast!'

Bridget poured herself more coffee. She said, 'There's one thing you seem to be forgetting. That boy-friend who everyone thinks is so innocent is still keeping himself hidden from the police. So why would that be, if he's in the clear?'

'Oh, Bridgie, now then!' Geoffrey said. 'He wants to talk to George, and that makes him fireproof. If he'd only kicked a cat he wouldn't want to do that.'

'So why doesn't he talk to him?'

'He's finding it difficult. Too many coppers around the place.'

'But if he's offering to give himself up anyway?'

'Perhaps he's hoping he won't have to, once he's talked to George.'

Bridget sniffed. 'I can't forget Rannoch Station. He wasn't acting like an innocent man there. He was desperate, taking risks, behaving like someone who knew he was done for. And I'm certain that if he'd really wanted to talk to George, he could have found an opportunity before now.'

'He could walk through that door any minute!'

'Then he needn't expect a cup of coffee.'

'You'd be the first to offer him one, my girl.'

'As it happened, I emptied the pot.'

Just at that moment the door bell did ring, but the early caller turned out to be Blayne. He came in making apologies, but with an odd expression on his long face.

'Ach, I'm grieved to be troublin' you over your breakfast, but some wee matter is aye turnin' up. And I'd be obliged – aye, downright grateful – if your man here could spare me a little of his time,'

Gently said, 'Have you heard from Fowler?'

Blayne hesitated. 'In a manner of speakin' – aye.'

'Then I'd best come along.'

'If you'll be so good. And if your lady and the folk here can spare you.'

'Of course he shall go!' Gabrielle said. 'Of that young man we have just been speaking. And he is safe and well?'

Blayne wriggled his shoulders. 'Somethin' of that sort, lady,' he said.

He hustled Gently out to the car that stood waiting. Its driver was the grim-faced Purdy. Gently waited till the doors were slammed and the engine started, then he turned to Blayne.

'Well?'

'Ach, here's a thing, man!' Blayne's face was working.

'Where did they find him?'

'Down by the loch. An angler it was who reported the body.'

'Strangled?'

'Na. His head was bashed in. And here's the rub o' the affair. The angler chiel was stayin' at The Highland, and he put it about there.'

'And the doctor . . .?'

'Long gone. I'm thinkin' there's no call to look much further.'

'You'll have put an alert out?'

Blayne nodded. 'The lads here noticed his car was missing. But it was over-late then, he'd booked out maybe an hour before.'

'The car is distinctive.'

'So it is. But this is bonnie country for hiding vehicles. You'll ken of your own knowin' how Knockie used to dispose of his.'

'That would leave him on foot.'

Blayne nodded again. 'And we're givin' special attention to the buses and trains. And maybe the ports and airports too, because we're dealin' with a laddie who does not lack siller. He'll no be a man for the braes, him, or for takin' off across the moor.'

'Perhaps a guest-house or small hotel.'

'Most likely that's where we'll be findin' him.'

They had driven down through the town and taken the turning to the car-park. There several patrol cars and an ambulance were gathered and at the gate a uniform man was posted. Purdy parked and they got out. Blayne led the way to the track to the loch.

'It was here . . .?'

'You'll soon be seein'.'

Down there, had been that evening stroll with Gabrielle. And down there men were standing about striped screens erected on the loch-shore. The same surgeon was in attendance as had been at the power station: it may have been the same ambulance-men.

'Can you give us an opinion?'

The surgeon shrugged. 'He's been in the water, so it's merely a guess. Say between eight and midnight last night – with a margin for error either way.'

'Can you tell us what hit him?'

'Something heavy and rough. My best guess is a lump of rock, but it could have been a club or some other blunt instrument.'

The body still lay as the angler had found it, half in the water, half on the beach, the yellow hair tangled, mouth gaping, eyes closed. It was clad in the shell-suit that Gently remembered, on its feet the same trainers. On the right side of the skull, a severe depressed fracture: Fowler had been facing the man who killed him. Clothes, hair were still drenched. At some time the body had been completely immersed. The spot was a few yards from the mouth of the river, of which the grey beach formed the delta. The spot where he had stood smoking, while Gabrielle had sat on the rock beside him . . .

The local sergeant approached them.

'We've given it a good look-over, sir,' he said to Blayne. 'We've found where the fisherman beached his boat and jammed around, but nothin' more.'

'A lump o' rock did it, the surgeon's sayin'.'

'There's nothin' of that sort around here.'

'Forbye a club or blunt instrument.'

'He could have disposed of it in the loch, sir.'

'A bash like yon would fetch blood.'

104

The sergeant shook his head. 'We have searched, sir. And if the job was done right here, then likely the loch-fret has washed it away.'

'Aye, more than likely.' Blayne looked at Gently. Gently said:

'Perhaps the search should continue upstream.'

'Upstream – aye. That's a canny notion!' Blayne turned to stare at the silent-moving river. 'Would that be possible?'

'Oh aye,' the sergeant said. 'That could be the way of it. You'll see how the current spreads out just here, and the bits o' rubbish it leaves on the beach.'

'But – a body, now?'

'Whyfore no', with all the water that's come down lately? It'll fetch rubbish the size o' that tree-bough, so I'm thinkin' it will not stop short at a body.'

'Ach, you're right!' Blayne said. 'Call in the men. We can finish the search down here later. I'm forgettin' the way it went before – this mannie has only one road with a body. No doubt he was thinkin' it would end up in the loch, and no' come to light this side of Christmas – well, he kens better now. So just be callin' the men in, sergeant.'

'It could have gone in at the falls, sir.'

'So fetch the men and start lookin'!'

The men dispersed down the loch-shore were assembled and given brief instruction by Blayne. Then they formed a line across the rough strath and began the upstream search. The photographer arrived and performed his function. The body was lifted and stretched away. From a pocket Blayne had taken a sodden wallet that offered identification and contained one ten-pound note.

'The poor young fule. And it was all for nothin', those high jinks at Rannoch Station. You're thinkin' he was this way, tryin' to find you?'

Gently nodded. 'And found someone else.'

'Ach, from the start my guts turned at that doctor! And we know well why he feared this laddie.'

'He could have given testimony that would have convicted him.'

'Aye. The lady was alive when the lad left the glen.'

'I think Collins may know that.'

'You've had a fresh word with him?'

'With Collins. And with someone who knows him.'

He related the encounters of the evening before. Blayne listened, his eyes glistening.

'So he was up the glen – we have two witnesses now! And the loon should talk now, when he hears of this caper. So the doctor's cooked. We have only to nab him. And just let him give trouble when I'm feelin' his collar.'

'Yesterday, I happened on some other information.'

He told Blayne of the conversation at The Bonnie Strathtudlem. This time Blayne was more impatient, and interrupted before Gently was through.

'Aye, I heard much of that from Glasgow, though they did not ken the trouble that Jamieson was brewin'. But there's aye bodies bein' fished from the Clyde, and I doubt they cannot lay that one to the doctor.'

'The body was never identified?'

'Na. It was too far gone even for prints. It was about the right size they was thinkin', but that's a', they could not connect it.'

'The teeth?'

'There was no head, man. The head they never found. Like it was chopped off by a ship's propeller, and is still rollin' around there at the bottom o' the Clyde. No, I'd like to hang that one on the doctor, but –' he looked down at the wallet – 'I'll just make myself content.'

'Another body. In another river.'

'So now we'll be makin' it firm and tight.'

The strath wasn't an easy area of search. Among the bracken and heather grew stunted birches, alders, willows, with here and there rocky outcrops and steep descents to the margin of the stream. On the right hand the ground rose sharply to the back of the buildings that lined the town's street, on the left, across the river, wooded braes closed in the view. Ahead, more trees concealed the bridge and the falls that lay beyond. And now the sun was beginning to strike warmly on the labourers at their work.

'No slacking, now!'

Blayne slapped irritably at a mosquito that had settled on his neck, and turned aside to prod a bush of bog myrtle that one of the searchers had passed by.

'Could we just be wastin' our time here, and he put it in up at the falls?'

Gently shook his head. 'Too many witnesses. It will have to be somewhere here.'

'Ach, must it be so important anyway, with everythin' else we have on the mannie?'

'Firm and tight is what you said. If there is evidence here, we need to have it.'

'Then I'll be holdin' this against him too,' Blayne said. 'Jings, there's no humanity in that fellow!'

But the search had only a few more minutes to go. Then there came a shout from the direction of the river: 'Over here, sir!' – and, in his eagerness, Blayne tripped over bracken and almost fell headlong.

'What have you got?'

'Just about the lot, sir.'

'Then stand back and let me see it!'

The searcher was standing by a low, level stretch of turf from which a vague track seemed to lead towards the town. The turf was scarred with savage heel-marks, one pair impressed at the very brink: and by it, as though carelessly cast aside, lay a nugget of granite the size of a small melon.

'Stand back, the lot o' you!'

Hissing through his teeth, Blayne stooped to examine the nugget. He felt in his pocket for a knife and, using the blade, turned the nugget a little aside.

'Will you just look . . .!'

Gently looked. Blood had congealed on a ragged edge of the nugget. Also, trapped in the blood, was a wisp of pale yellow hair.

'Evidence, you was sayin'?'

Gently nodded.

'Ach, if I could get my hands on that doctor!'

'We shall need casts of those heel-prints, too.'

'Aye, and him travellin' with just one pair of shoes.'

Blayne straightened and cast his eyes round the spot. Birches, willows formed a screen around it. Above, one could see the roofs of the street and the low sheds of the garage and a motor-caravan parked behind it. Then there was the track leading into the rough and striking a line towards the town.

'Sergeant!'

The local man stepped forward.

'Would you ken where this path runs to, now?'

'It runs up to the town, sir. The fishermen use it. It comes out by the phone-box beside the garage.'

'Beside – the garage?'

'That's right, sir. Between the garage and that pair o' shops.'

Blayne's eyes gleamed. 'Then we might just have a witness – if that scruffy devil was not round at The Clachan!' He beckoned to Purdy. 'Take over, man, and make sure it's a' done by the book. I'm thinkin' we'll have that doctor in such a bind that he'll ne'er see the outside of Barlinnie again.'

Gently said, 'The pump-attendant lives in that caravan?'

'Just there,' Blayne said. 'Just there.'

He led the way. The track improved as it left the trees and the scrub behind, eventually to become a steep lane pushing up between the garage-yard and a house-end. Above the wall of the yard peered the motor-caravan, an ancient coach-built Commer, and ahead, at street-level, stood the old-fashioned red phone-box: and just across the street, The Highland Arms. Blayne paused to stare at this ominous conjunction.

'The poor, daft laddie! He must have been after makin' his call. And the doctor sees him. And he sees the doctor. And he takes off down into the rough. Ach, you can see it a' – and he had but to have stepped quietly off that train.'

Gently shrugged. The room Angus had occupied looked straight down at the red phone-box.

'You checked with the hotel?'

'Aye, first thing. They think he went out around eight. And he was not back in till after ten. It a' fits him like a glove.'

'Yet . . . he waited till this morning to book out.'

'Because he thought the body was safe away! And it would

have put a finger straight on him if he had rushed off, last thing at night. Na, he was playin' it canny till that daft angler put it about. There could be no hangin' about then. He was out o' there by half-eight.'

Gently nodded. 'And there's just a chance . . .'

'Come on – let's grab that scruffy body!'

They found the attendant at his post, filling the tank of someone's Peugeot. He gave them a quick glance through his greasy locks but went on with his task. The customer paid, the cash was rung up, and a token handed through the window. Then, with a glance at the office, he advanced cautiously towards them.

'You're wantin' somethin' then – you havena laid hold of the doctor yet?'

'None o' your cheek, now!' Blayne said. 'But a straight answer – what were you doin' with yourself last night?'

'What was I – ?'

'Were you in your van, man, or were you puttin' it away at The Clachan?'

'Ach, that!' He gave his hair a jerk. 'Maybe I was there while a couple o' drams.'

'And when would that have been?'

'Weel . . . when I finished here. Hector will tell you just when.'

'Then you came back here?'

'Aye, but dinna ask me –'

'Were you back in your van before eight?'

He was, it appeared. There had been a TV programme he had wished to see and which started at that time. So, after a ritual visit to The Clachan, he had returned to the garage and his van. Though:

'It wasna dead on eight, you ken . . . I maybe missed the first five minutes o' ma programme.'

He took them to the van. From its none-too-clean windows one looked directly down towards the river, but the view of it was obscured by the growth of birches and willows. Through the windscreen one saw the phone-box and the beginning of the lane. There was also a view of The Highland Arms extending to the entrance: and the room above it.

'Now, my mannie! You have a braw prospect, and we're wantin' to hear what you saw last night. You were back here at eight or near it, you're tellin' us, so we'll just be takin' it from there.'

'But whit's it aboot – what should I be seein'?'

'For a start, was there any chiel hangin' round the phone-box?'

'Ach, they're always hangin' round there!'

'But someone you kenned?'

Scruffy Jock gazed at him.

'Well?'

'Is it – would it be the doctor you're meanin'?'

'The doctor,' Blayne said. 'You saw the doctor?'

'Noo, not exactly saw him!' Scruffy Jock said hastily. 'It was when I was watchin' ma programme, you ken, but there was some loon went by down below. I didna turn round, didna look at him, just caught a glim from the corner o' ma eye. But he'd be tall, to show over the wall, an' he was wearin' dark clothes.'

'Dark clothes, was he?' Blayne slid a look at Gently. 'And about what time was it when he went by?'

'It wasna long after I sat down, maybe not yet half after eight.'

'And he was in a hurry – this man in dark clothes?'

'Mind, I'm not sayin' it was the doctor!'

'But he did not hang about?'

'Weel – na. The way he slipped by, he could have been runnin'.'

'Runnin' after another man?'

'I couldna just say.'

'A man you were seein' earlier – say, beside the phone-box?'

Scruffy Jock hesitated. 'Maybe I was seein' one, but I canna preceesely bring him to mind. Sometimes they're queuein' up down there, an' it was the box yon I had my e'e on.'

'But – you did see one?'

'Aye, maybe.'

'And like you're noticin' the colour o' his hair.'

'Aye, perhaps. Now you come to mention it.'

'And it was not just black?'

'It wasna . . .' Scruffy Jock was staring at him. 'Ach, to

110

goodness! You wouldna be tellin' me it was that laddie who was out there?'

'What are you tellin' me?' Blayne said.

'Ach, no! An' here you are, askin' – an' you've laddies down there . . .' He snatched at his dangling locks. 'What's goin' on – what happened last night?'

Blayne stared back with narrowed eyes. 'You ken that somethin' did happen?' he said.

'Weel, would you be here – an' those laddies –'

'It is not just that,' Blayne said, 'is it?'

Scruffy Jock pulled his stubbly face aside. He stared down towards the river, where several policemen were visible. He dragged on the greasy hair.

'Well?'

'I jist thought it was the callants – they're aye fulin' down there! An' I never guessed – why would I? – that anythin' out o' the way was happenin'. An' you're tellin' me . . .'

'I'm tellin' you nothing.'

'But losh man, I must have heard it goin' on! An' I never guessed . . .' He dragged harder. 'Which o' them was it – the doctor, or him?'

'Just get on,' Blayne said softly.

Scruffy Jock gazed through his hair. 'So I'm hearin' some shoutin' down there, aren't I? Like the callants were at their larks.'

'You saw nothing?'

'Ach, no! It was down there, behind the bushes. An' I'm cussin' them to maself an' willin' them to have done. But they was at it for a while, dingin' away, an' I was half in a mind to go an' sort them out. Then there was a bit o' a splashin', an' after that the shoutin' stopped.'

'You heard a splash?'

'Aye. So I thought. I'm takin' it the callants had blundered in. An' that's a', there's no more noise, an' I'm blessin' maself that it's over an' done.'

Blayne said, 'Was this before or after the mannie went by?'

'After, it was. We'd got to the news.'

'And you would not have seen him come up again?'

Scruffy Jock hesitated, then shook his long locks.

111

'Right,' Blayne said. 'You're a braw cratur, Jock, and what you're handin' us is bonnie information. So we'll just be having you along to the station and gettin' it safe and sound on paper.'

'But whit's it about – which o' them was it?'

'You'll be hearin',' Blayne said. 'And maybe guessin'. But for the moment you'll be giving your statement, and puttin' your cross to it before a witness.'

'Ach!' Scruffy Jock stared resentfully. 'Then I'll be gettin' leave from Mr Frazer. He's had to fill two cars himself a'ready, an' he's not in the best o' tempers this mornin'.'

He went; they climbed down from the van. After a few steps, Blayne glanced at Gently.

'Would you not say now we had it wrapped up, or as near as the Prosecutor will be wishin'?'

Gently shrugged. 'He fed you the doctor.'

'You're thinkin' so?'

Gently nodded.

'But you ken, he would not swear to him.'

'Perhaps that's what I mean.'

Blayne stared at him, then away. 'Aweel, I may have led him a wee,' he said. 'And it's no great secret who we fancy. So it's just a tall man wearin' dark clothin', and that's what the jury will be seein' in the dock. But the rest will be just routine, I'm thinkin'.'

'It certainly looks that way,' Gently said.

'Ach, but it's a foul business,' Blayne said, his eye straying towards the phone-box. 'The lady you may think was askin' for it, she'd been playin' these games for aye. But not the young lad. He was just led astray. No cause for him to wind up in the river.'

'He should have picked a different phone-box.'

'He was not to know. He would not ken where the doctor was stayin'. It was there and handy, and maybe he was thinkin' that below would be a good place to talk to you.'

Gently nodded. 'But, instead . . .'

Blayne gave him a quick look. 'You're no' blaming yourself?'

'Perhaps not. But it's hard to forget that it was because of me he came back here.'

Blayne rocked his shoulders. 'He set himself up, man! It was not you put the idea in his head. He was about followin' his own fulish notions, and by bad luck they fetched him to this spot. You cannot be blamed.'

'Yes, that's the logic.'

'So mind you stick with the logic, man. And here's Jock, the ruffian. You would not be wantin' to sit in while we are takin' him down?'

Gently shook his head. 'I'll get back.'

'Aye, well. It's routine from now on, I'm thinkin'.'

Gently watched Scruffy Jock led away, then walked slowly back up the street. He stood a while at the bridge, watching the water, the water rushing down to join the loch. Just after nine the tragedy must have happened. When he was sitting with Gabrielle outside The Bridge of Eden Hotel. Watching the mist grow on the loch. While the water came down, as now, from the falls. An evening of such peace, a peace so solemn. And . . . yet. Gently stuck a pipe in his mouth and walked on. He glanced towards the mill. The green Volvo was parked there, and Collins was seeing customers out at the door. Their eyes met. Collins cut short his chatter and hastily disappeared into the mill. Gently paused to light his pipe, then continued on his way to the cottage.

9

'I know it sounds pious,' Bridget said. 'But someone should say it just the same. The wages of sin and all that. Those two asked for it, and now they've got it.'

The post-mortem had taken place on the sunny terrace, with the view of the town and the ben before them. There they had sat with beakers of coffee and tried to absorb this latest harrowing development. It was the wrong sort of day for it. There wasn't a cloud. The sun shone peerlessly from a tender blue sky. Squealing swifts were chasing below, jackdaws were exchanging domestic caws, and every detail of the ben stood out with luminous precision. In such a setting tragedy was out of place, seemed somehow like a tale told by an idiot. How could hatred and violence exist alongside a prospect so delectable?

Perhaps Gabrielle had been the most shaken by the news that Gently had had to relate. For some moments she had stared at him in silence. Then she had given a little, smothered sob.

'He did not deserve that!'

Geoffrey had winced. 'It was a bit extreme!'

Bridget said, 'He was not exactly innocent. And it would never have happened if he hadn't run away.'

'Oh, I don't know, Bridgie.'

'Well, it wouldn't. He should have stood up to things like a man.'

'I might have done the same thing, in his position.'

'Oh no you wouldn't, Geoffrey. Not you.'

'But I could understand it.'

'You're just being a lawyer. It has all happened because he had a guilty conscience.'

'But he did not deserve that!' Gabrielle repeated. 'He is a foolish young man, that is all. He is kicking over the traces, yes, and suddenly his world has come to an end.'

'He brought it on himself. Just as she did.'

'But that lady is knowing what she is doing. It is she one must blame.'

'I'll go along with that,' Geoffrey said.

Bridget sniffed. 'Well, there's not much doubt now, if the doctor has really done a bunk. I suppose we have to accept that he's the culprit. Though I must say I find it hard to believe it of him.'

'He had motive, Bridgie. And opportunity.'

'Oh, you don't have to rub it in. But it's still not clear that he strangled his wife. It could just as well have been her lover or the fellow from the mill.'

'Oh, not my poor Mr Collins!' Gabrielle said.

'He's mixed up in it somehow,' Bridget said. 'And now there are two witnesses who saw him up the glen. There's no getting away from that.'

'They are seeing a car – it could be some other!'

'The police haven't found another one yet.'

'I think we have to accept it,' Geoffrey said. 'He was up the glen. Though that doesn't mean he was in any way involved.'

But Gabrielle wasn't giving up the antique dealer. 'This man I am talking to,' she said. 'He is gentle, he is kind. It is not possible he would do such a thing.'

'Say a rush of blood,' Geoffrey said.

'No, never! He is not capable. But the doctor, ha, yes – was he not suspect of killing his partner?'

'Just suspect,' Geoffrey said. 'But you have a point.'

'So now again, both times, he is on the spot. And who is running away this time, yes? It is that wicked man, not my poor Mr Collins.'

Geoffrey looked at Gently. 'I suppose there is no doubt?'

'There can always be room for it.' Gently shrugged.

'But not very much?'

'There's a strong case.'

'And from you, that's as good as saying yes,' Geoffrey said. 'Sorry, Bridgie!'

115

Bridget drank coffee. She said, 'Then at least that lets George out. He doesn't have to hang about waiting for messages or holding Blayne's hand any longer. He can bear to leave them to catch the doctor and perhaps to interrogate him when caught. So I will risk making myself unpopular by repeating that we are still on holiday.'

'Oh!' Geoffrey said.

'Well?'

'It is hard to forget that young man,' Gabrielle said.

Bridget sniffed. 'We saw him just once. And then in a light not exquisitely favourable.'

'But . . . he is dead.'

'And we can't resurrect him.'

'Take it easy, Bridgie!' Geoffrey said. 'It is a bit of a shock.'

'So, the sooner we forget it the better. And we won't do that by hanging round here.' She got up. 'I'm going to pack a picnic,' she said. 'It's too late now to go anywhere special. But there are plenty of spots round about away from the town and from importunate policemen.'

'Oh, not up the glen!' Gabrielle pleaded. 'Sooner, it shall be the braes of the ramping hizzie.'

'George may choose the spot,' Bridget said. 'Just as long as it's peaceful and away from everywhere.'

'We could climb the ben,' Geoffrey said. 'It would seem to qualify.'

But Bridget didn't seem to think that deserved an answer.

In the end they chose the back road skirting the loch, which didn't involve driving through the town; they had merely to cross the bridge and make a turn by The Clachan's car-park. Soon the town was lost behind trees and the road climbing to its view of the loch, and if there was yet activity at the mouth of the river that, too, was mercifully screened. It called for a drive of little more than two miles to bring them to a spot that earned Bridget's approval. Here, a forestry ride joined the road and offered adequate parking for the two cars, with the prospect of the loch spread below them and beyond it the ben and its supporting hills. Rover and

Jaguar, they pulled in, and parked with care on the rugged surface.

'It was up here, on that first day . . .'

Gabrielle made a little face: it was on that same road that the policeman had accosted them, suspecting them to be Fowler and Mrs Angus.

'That was a few miles further on.'

'It is still the same road . . . the same view.'

'At the time, we were amused.'

'And now . . . both of them.'

Gently laid his hand on her arm.

'I've brought a rug for a table-cloth,' Bridget said. 'Geoffrey, we'll have it at that spot in the shade. Really, when the sun gets going up here it's just as bad as the south of France.'

'I expect the hills trap the heat, old girl.'

'Well, it isn't what one expects in Scotland.'

Clearly Bridget was edgy too. It showed in the way she tossed out the picnic. Today it was a simple meal of fruit and cheese, followed by wedges of buttered bannoch, and washed down with rather strong coffee from the pair of thermos flasks. It was eaten very largely in silence while people stared at the impressive view, the chequered braes, the sun-struck peak, the tiny movements of vehicles on the road across the loch. The pines beside them yielded a resinous fragrance and were the home of numerous twittering birds. Behind, the ride rose steeply through the trees, then took a turn and disappeared.

At last the too-silent meal was over, and Geoffrey sighed and stretched out in the grass. He said:

'It's no good, Bridgie. One has to think about it. Even away from it all up here.'

'I don't care,' Bridget said. 'One doesn't have to talk about it. One can talk about it. One can talk about the view.'

'It doesn't stop one thinking, though.' Geoffrey cradled his head. 'Just now I'm thinking about the doctor. I mean, a man like him, in a whacking great Merc. How could he vanish from the face of the earth?'

'That's a matter for the police. Not us.'

'But it doesn't stop you wondering,' Geoffrey said. 'One tries to put one's self in his position and to work it out from there. What would you do?'

'First,' Gabrielle said, 'you would hide the car away, yes?'

'That would be my first move,' Geoffrey said. 'And the sooner I could get it under cover the better.'

'So then, he will not be going very far.'

Geoffrey nodded. 'The first place handy would be my choice. As soon as the police have discovered I'm missing every road in the district will be under surveillance.'

'Then, when the car is hidden?'

'I'd sit tight. I can't use the car or public transport. So I'll wait for the heat to go off a little while I plan what my next move is to be.'

'You will need food.'

'I may have thought of that, and laid some in before I took off.'

'In your car is a radio and a telephone, ha?'

'Just so. I shall have intelligence of what the police are doing.'

'So you keep sitting tight, yes?'

'Yes. Until I spot a weakness in the net set to catch me.'

'Oh,' Bridget said, 'what utter nonsense. Do you think the police haven't thought of this already? Of course they have. And where could it be, this wonderful hideout next-door to Kinleary?'

'That's just what I'm wondering,' Geoffrey grinned. 'A handy spot, away from it all. A couple of miles or so out of town. Off a minor road. With next to no traffic.'

'Oh, how stupid! You can't mean it.'

'Seems the ideal place,' Geoffrey said. 'Just up the ride and he's home and dry. It would have taken him only ten minutes to get here.'

'You aren't serious.' Bridget cast a hasty glance up the ride. 'Tell him, George. The police would have checked a place like this already.'

'Probably not yet,' Gently smiled. 'The doctor has only been missing for a few hours. No doubt in time they'll get round to it. Unless they pick him up first.'

'You see?' Geoffrey said. 'We could be sitting on him, Bridgie. His Merc could be just up there, round the bend. I vote we

118

explore. It's our duty as citizens. And I might be able to persuade him to engage me as his counsel.'

'You see? You're not serious!'

'Never more so.'

'We could explore just a little,' Gabrielle said. 'It may be we shall not find the doctor, but deer we may see, and perhaps a wild-cat.'

'George, tell him this is nonsense!'

Gently shook his head. 'Perhaps not entirely nonsense,' he said. 'Though, unless the doctor was equipped with bolt-cutters, I can't see him getting through the gate up there.'

In the end, when the picnic was cleared away, they did set out to explore the ride, with Bridget sticking close to the eager Geoffrey and Gently and Gabrielle tagging behind. And in fact the doctor would not have needed bolt-cutters: the gate was secured only by a rusty chain without a lock, while there was some evidence, in a dried-out puddle, that a vehicle might have passed that way recently.

'We're on his trail, folk – or someone's!'

Geoffrey pressed on towards the bend. But Gabrielle, who had paused at the gate to gaze back at the view, suddenly snatched at Gently's arm.

'Look!'

Down at the road a car had passed, and now was easing back again towards the parking. The driver seemed to hesitate. Then he reversed in. The car was a green Volvo estate.

'It is him. Perhaps he wishes to talk!'

A forlorn figure had climbed out and was staring towards them.

Gently said, 'You go on. And try to think up some excuse to tell Bridget.'

Dennis Collins looked like a man who hadn't slept very well. His lined, colourless cheeks had a drawn appearance and his blue eyes were set in a stare. He stood by his car as Gently approached and seemed inclined to shrink towards it. Gently paused a couple of yards off, looked at the car, looked at the man.

119

'You wanted a word with me?'

Collins nodded, as though he couldn't trust himself to speak. Then he made a jerky gesture towards the Rover. 'I – I was passing. I thought that was your car!'

'You had business up here?'

'Yes – business. I had a buying address, but the man wasn't in. Then, as I came back . . . I could see it was you up there, with Mrs Gently.'

'And you had something to tell me?'

'Something – oh lord!' Collins snatched his face away and stared at the loch. 'He's done it again, hasn't he. And it must have been just after that –'

Gently said, 'We're talking about Angus?'

'Yes. Who else.'

'And you know something about what happened last night?'

'That man is dangerous. And when I heard on the news –' Collins slammed his fists down on the car.

Gently gazed at him for a moment. Then he said, 'Perhaps you'll tell me where you were yesterday evening.'

'I . . . where?'

'When I visited you last night the bonnet of your car was still a little warm.'

Collins jerked round to him. 'You felt my car?'

'Just a habit policemen have.'

'Oh my God. And you really believe – ?'

'It might help to know where you were. And when.'

Collins stared with horrified eyes. 'But I wasn't anywhere – nowhere at all! I stayed late at the mill, that's all, writing cheques and dealing with correspondence. Then I drove home. If the car was still warm it was because I was late, nothing else.'

'You were at the mill till when?'

'Till eight, it must have been. You're not for one moment suggesting – ?'

'And you returned down the street as usual?'

'There isn't any other way to get to mine!'

'At around eight o'clock?'

'Yes. Around then.'

Gently said, 'I'd like you to think about that. Who you passed.

120

What you saw. Anything the smallest bit unusual. Or perhaps not unusual at all.'

'But –'

'Take it from the top of the street. Did you notice anyone crossing the bridge?'

'There are always people crossing the bridge –'

'Perhaps someone you knew?'

Collins stared helplessly.

Gently said, 'Try to remember, because this could be important. Around eight o'clock is the time in which we are interested. We need to check the movements of certain people. And you were passing down the street at that time.'

'But I wasn't thinking –'

'Try.'

'If you mean Angus –'

'Yes?'

Collins shook his head. 'I simply didn't. And I certainly wouldn't have forgotten him.'

'Then anyone else?'

'No. I'm sorry.'

'Would you have noticed if anyone was using the phone-box?'

Collins hesitated. 'There was someone in it. A woman. And someone else waiting to use it.'

'Someone else?'

'I don't know! A young fellow. He had his back to me.'

'Was he wearing a hat?'

'No. Now you mention it – oh, my God!' Collins' eyes were suddenly large. 'Is that where – could it have been?'

'A young man with fair hair?'

Collins nodded. 'He was standing in the entry. And it was down there . . . oh, this is terrible!'

'But no sign of the doctor.'

'No. Not then!'

'Not then?'

'No. Later. He came to my house.'

'To . . . your house?'

'And it must have been straight after. Straight after he'd killed that poor young fellow.'

* * *

Collins swung round to stare at the loch again, at the sunny braes on the opposite shore. Gently glanced up the ride. But, as yet, there was no sign of the explorers returning. He said:

'Let's get this clear. Angus paid you a visit. The time of that visit could be critical. When was it?'

Collins groaned. 'After. It had to be after when he got there.'

'But – more precisely?'

'I can't be certain! I made myself a meal when I got in. Then I was marking a sales-catalogue. That's what I was doing when he rang the bell.'

'Nine. Ten?'

'Nearer ten. He hadn't gone long when you turned up. That's why –'

'Why you put the bolt on?'

'Yes! I was scared. I think I must have sensed –'

'He had been belligerent?'

Collins nodded. 'You saw what he was like before. This time it was worse. He really scared me. And if I'd known then what I know now . . .'

'The same accusations.'

'It was more than that! He was trying to bully me into a confession. He said it was only a matter of time before you – the police – got the evidence they needed and arrested me. He said I might as well confess now, because it was going to happen, and then you would let him go back to his patients. I tried to reason with him. It was no use. I felt that any moment he was going to turn violent.'

'And this is why I found you in such a nervous state?'

'Yes! I felt sure you had come to arrest me. I thought he must have gone straight to you and convinced you of my guilt, and that was that.'

Gently said, 'Because . . . you had been Mrs Angus's lover?'

Collins kept staring at the braes. He said, 'I could go on denying it, couldn't I? And I wasn't the first. And certainly not the last.'

Gently shrugged; Collins stared. A white bird, a gull, winged up from the loch. Collins said:

122

'It was after Molly died. I felt so lonely. I couldn't help it.'

'And that led to your leaving Bearsden?'

'Yes . . . he made it impossible for me. My best customers were patients of his. I would have gone broke if I'd stayed on.'

'And the lady wasn't sympathetic?'

Collins' mouth puckered. 'She wasn't the person I'd taken her for. I suppose I should have known better. She admitted quite openly that she'd been unfaithful to her first husband, too.'

'To Dr Jamieson.'

Collins nodded. 'I never knew him. That was before my time at Bearsden. But I heard all the scandal of course. And the odd way he suddenly vanished.' He looked quickly at Gently. 'Would it have been possible?'

Gently said, 'And this lady you saw again at The Clachan?'

'Yes. I did.'

'With her latest boy-friend?'

Collins looked away again, pressed his fists hard against the Volvo. Gently said:

'It was you up the glen on Monday, wasn't it? It can't matter if you admit to it now. You had seen her, and you couldn't help following her up there. And there you saw her again. Behind the gorses.'

'Oh lord, you're worse than he was!'

'Collins, there's no point in denying it further. It can only leave you under suspicion. It is in your own interest to tell us the truth.'

'But then I would have to admit –'

'Yes?'

'No, it's no good! I'm not a fool. Once I'd admitted that you would pull me in straight away.'

'We just want the truth, Collins.'

'Yes, he knew that. He wanted me to say it.'

'We want your testimony. Nothing else.'

Collins beat his fists on the Volvo. 'I wasn't there – I was in the mill – I was in the mill all day! And I wouldn't have followed that woman anywhere, even if I had known where to look.'

Gently said, 'We have two witnesses.'

'Then they saw a car. But it wasn't mine. I was where I said, all day, minding my business in the mill.'

123

'It leaves a mark against you.'

Collins groaned and gave another thump to the Volvo. He stared wretchedly at the loch, the braes, at the gull that still glided above them.

'Perhaps I would be better off inside.'

Gently watched him, but said nothing.

'He's killed twice. It could be three times. And he certainly has it in for me.' Collins hesitated. 'There isn't . . . there can't be any doubt, can there?'

Gently said, 'The investigation is not yet complete.'

'But . . . he'd have been around there. And now he's cleared off!'

Gently shrugged. Collins stared at him, large-eyed. Gently said:

'And that's all you have to tell me?'

'All! I wanted to let you know about him threatening me last night. That's something, isn't it? About his state of mind – and straight after what he did to that young man?'

'And that's . . . all.'

'Yes. All!'

'Your account of your movements on Monday is to stand?'

'Oh God!' Collins said. 'I've had enough. I wish now I'd simply driven straight past.' He wrenched open the car door and jumped in.

'Wait,' Gently said.

'I've had enough!'

Gently said, 'You are to report to the police station when you get back and to give them a statement of what you have just told me. Is that understood?'

'Understood,' Collins said bitterly. 'Anything else?'

'You haven't buckled your seat-belt.'

Collins buckled it and took off. Gently watched the Volvo disappear. Only moments later there was a hail from the top of the ride and he turned to see the exploring party negotiating the gate. He went up to meet them.

'You should have come too,' Bridget said. 'We saw six deer, and one of them had antlers. Then there was a bird which I thought was an eagle, but which Geoffrey said was probably a buzzard.'

124

'No sign of a Mercedes?'

'Just a Land Rover,' Geoffrey grinned. 'The Forestry are clearing some scrub up there. But you're a fine one! What's the score? I take it they've reached half-time by now.'

'The score . . .?'

'The World Cup Match. Isn't that what you stayed behind to listen to?'

'Oh, that,' Gently said. 'It was very dull. I gave it up and went to stare at the loch.'

Gabrielle looked, but said nothing.

'I think there may be some coffee left,' Bridget said.

Later on, when they had returned to the cottage, Gently's excuse was a purchase of tobacco. An understanding Gabrielle stayed to keep Bridget company: Geoffrey was already sketching in the garden. Gently found Blayne at the police station. He was frowning over a sheet of statement-paper.

'Is that Collins' statement?'

'Aye, it is. And I could have wished to have been here when the chiel makin' it. If it's the way he says, and no mistake, the doctor must have moved fast after seein' to Fowler.'

'May I see it?'

Blayne handed him the statement. It followed roughly the conversation he had had with Collins. Emphasized was Angus's threatening bearing and his attempts to force Collins to confess. Gently related his encounter with Collins.

'Fine, you did fine,' Blayne said. 'And you think it's the truth he's puttin' down here – he did get a late-night call from the doctor?'

'I think he probably did.'

'But it's cuttin' it close, man, if the timings we have are correct. And you'd be thinkin' that even a mannie like the doctor would be needin' a breather after bloody murder.'

Gently nodded. 'It may have acted as a spur. He knew we must have a few doubts about Collins.'

'Aye, he was up the glen, no doubt. And he was there with opportunity.'

'And still – denies it.'

Blayne gazed at the statement. 'You would not be thinkin' – just a little – that we're bein' over-hard on the doctor? That maybe the truth is lyin' somewhere between, and that neither one nor the other is so dooms innocent?'

Gently thought about it, but shook his head. 'One man was responsible for both those killings.'

'I'm thinkin' this way,' Blayne said. 'Just suppose yon Collins was the laddie behind the bushes, and the doctor kens it, and kens we'll be gettin' round to him in the end.'

'So?'

'Then the doctor sees Fowler, and his dander is up, and what happened does happen – and it'll be Collins takin' the blame for that too, just so be it the doctor can get him to confess.'

'So . . . the doctor hastens round to Collins'.'

'Aye. That would give us the explanation.'

'But, if Collins wasn't the laddie behind the bushes?'

'Ach!' Blayne said. 'Then we're back where we were before. And the truth is he's a little light on motive, as I'm sure you'll be rubbin' in.'

Gently nodded. 'But I'll go along with you so far. The doctor's behaviour was a little unexpected. After what had happened a more likely reaction would have been an attempt to provide an alibi.' He paused. 'I take it there is no news of him?'

'Na, not a whisper,' Blayne said. 'The net is spread for him far and wide, but it's like the devil had vanished off into space. Aye, but it's early days yet.'

'He'll need lodgings for the night. Unless he sleeps in his car.'

'Leave it with me,' Blayne said. 'The traps are set a' around. He has but to show that porridge-face once and he'll be snatched before he can blink.'

'Meanwhile, did you have any luck with that other green Volvo?'

'Ach, no. The fellow had another errand, in Stirling.'

'Which leaves us with Collins.'

'Was there ever any doubt?' Blayne smoothed the statement on the desk at which he was sitting. 'He was up there, whatever he says, and he could tell us more than he's come out with yet. And I'll be for keepin' my eye on that chiel, you need have no fear of that.'

126

'Yet . . . just suppose he's telling only the truth?'

'Ach, get away!' Blayne said. 'Was there ever a dealer in antiques who did?'

Gently shrugged, and sighed. But he didn't dispute the point.

10

Where, in that neighbourhood, could one conceal a car? At the bridge Gently paused. He leaned against the stone parapet and let his eye wander over the scene. Because Geoffrey had been right. When Angus left the hotel he had known that his time was short, that he had been lucky to get away at all after the discovery of Fowler's body had been reported. His car was distinctive. He couldn't drive far before a police patrol caught up with him. His need was to get into cover quickly, to conceal the car, conceal himself. The ride where they had picnicked offered just such a bolt-hole – or would have done if the Forestry hadn't got there first! And others there must be, as yet unsifted, in the network of glens round about . . .

Five roads led out of Kinleary, the first being the link to the main route north and south. That connected with Balmagussie and Stirling in one direction and Fort William and the Isles in the other, passing two stations that gave rail access alternatively to Glasgow or Mallaig. But patrols could be expected on that road, and the stations would quickly be covered: if Angus had gone that way he would have been picked up long since. Then there was the main road up the loch to Torlinnhead and the parallel back road where they had picnicked; another minor road, leading to the north-south highway, and . . . the long, twisting cul-de-sac up Glen Eden. Was that a credible prospect? Gently let his mind dwell on it, on every reach of that fatal road. Twice Angus had been along there, so he would know what it had to offer. And a fascination with it might exist for him, might draw him in that direction. Assuredly it would get him off the principal through-routes and into cover the soonest of all, unless . . . Gently's eye wandered back to the town. Was it just possible that Angus had never left it? That during his sojourn at The Highland Arms he had located some bolt-hole in the town itself?

'Have you no' found him then, the slippery doctor?'

Scruffy Jock was passing on his way to The Clachan. There was a gleam in the deep-set eyes that surveyed Gently through the tangle of hair. Gently said:

'Hang on a moment!'

'At your sairvice,' Scruffy Jock said agreeably. 'I'm aye one for assistin' the polis. Are you wantin' me to swear, now, it was the doctor I saw?'

Gently eyed him. 'Just tell me this,' he said. 'You'll be a man who knows the town well. If you were wanting to hide a stolen car here, where would you conceal it?'

'Ach, now then!' Scruffy Jock said. 'I never have dealin's wi' that manner o' gear. I'm just an honest laddie aboot the garage. What's to do, then – ha'e you lost your car?'

'Never mind about that! Where would you hide it?'

'A hot car, you're sayin'?'

Gently nodded.

'Where the polis wouldn't find it?'

'Just that.'

'It wouldna just be, now – ach, no!' The sunken eyes were cunning. 'It couldna just be a grey Mercedes?'

Gently stared at him.

'Aweel,' Scruffy Jock said. 'There's a braw notion for ye! An' the polis huntin' far an' wide – an' him still hangin' on here, you're thinkin'.'

Gently said, 'If you'll just answer my question.'

'Richt awa'!' Scruffy Jock said. 'But there isna that many places in the toon to hide a car, ootside a private garage or some such biggin.'

'Are there any lock-ups?'

Scruffy Jock shook his head. 'There isna much call for them in Leary. An' I kenna no empty houses wi' garages whilk the chiel might have used. There's an auld barn oot by the power station, but that's o'erlooked by the office, an' a bit o' a shed on the playin'-field, but the weans are in an' oot a' the time.'

129

'Perhaps some waste ground with suitable cover?'

'Aye.' He considered it with narrowed eyes. 'You could drop a car doon by me, but I wouldna say you could find it cover. Then there's some rough ground ahint The Clachan. An' a loanin' through the birks just along here.'

'But nothing very likely.'

He shook his head again. 'Some nosey body would find it for sure. Na, it's a garage the man would be needin' if he's to hide it awa' in Leary.' The shadowed eyes were keen. 'But is it a fac', then? You have a reason for thinkin' he's still in the toon?'

Gently said, 'We're talking about stolen cars. And perhaps it's time you went for your drink.'

'Ach, but I shallna be gabbin' aboot it – an' I could be spottin' the slippery cratur!'

Gently stared, but said nothing.

'Weel, have it your way,' Scruffy Jock said. 'But I kent from the first he was meanin' trouble, that day he came stormin' into the forecourt. An' if it will help put a spoke in his wheel, a' you have to do is gi'e me a wink.'

Gently didn't give him a wink. He was no longer looking at Scruffy Jock. A figure had just then come out of the mill, slamming and locking the door behind him. To Scruffy Jock, Gently said:

'On your way!'

'Aye, I will. But you'll no' be forgettin' –'

Reluctantly, Scruffy Jock continued a few steps across the bridge. Collins approached. In his mien there was agitation. He caught sight of Gently and hastened towards him. His face was pale and he was trembling: he pushed out a hand towards the parapet to steady himself. He blurted:

'This is terrible! I've just had Angus on the phone.'

'Angus!'

'He was threatening me. Now he's accusing me of killing Fowler too! And he swears that, if I don't confess, he won't be responsible for what he does.'

Gently nodded towards the loitering garage-attendant. 'Perhaps we should discuss this somewhere more private . . .?'

'No. No!' Collins had spotted the scruffy one. 'He's the man I want, don't you see?'

'The man you want . . .?'

'He can prove my innocence! It was he who delivered my car. And if it wasn't there when the police say it was, it couldn't have been me who was up the glen.'

Gently shook his head. 'I think you're catching at straws.'

'But I've got to prove it. That man is after me! He as much as said there'd be a third victim if I didn't confess to killing his wife.'

'Just the same . . .'

But Collins wasn't to be thwarted. He dodged round Gently to the startled garageman. Spreading his hands pleadingly, he declared:

'Jock, my friend! You're going to help me, aren't you?'

'Weel, Mr Collins . . .' Scruffy Jock looked baffled.

'I've always seen you right, haven't I?'

'Aye, you have –'

'You've never found me mean?'

'Ach no, Mr Collins! You're aye free-handed.'

'Jock, you've got to tell the truth about delivering my car – that it wasn't what you said when the police asked you. It was after lunch, not before. Or perhaps you went late to your lunch on Monday.'

Scruffy Jock gazed helplessly at Collins, at Gently. He sought inspiration in a tug at his locks. He said, 'You ken I would like to be helpin' you, Mr Collins – a free-handed mannie like yoursel' –'

'Then say it – you delivered the car after lunch!'

'Aye, I'd be for sayin' that. If I could.'

'Then you did?'

'Weel, if I'd lunched early –'

'It was after twelve o'clock, man – nearer one.'

Scruffy Jock twisted himself tormentedly. 'If it just rested wi' me now, you ken . . .'

'But it does rest with you!'

'Ach, but it doesna. The polis were no' content wi' the word o' a puir laddie. They was for askin' Mr Frazer too, an' I canna just be callin' my boss a liar.'

131

Collins gazed at him. 'But it has to be wrong!'

'If you could have a wee word, now, wi' Mr Frazer . . .'

'That car wasn't there. It's my only hope!'

Regretfully, Scruffy Jock shook his tangling locks.

'Oh my God.'

Collins turned from him to stare at the water rushing below. Scruffy Jock gave Gently a sheepish look, seeming not to know whether to go or stay. Gently said:

'There is no question, is there? Mr Collins' car was delivered at noon?'

'Ach, yes. I darena say other. I dropped it off before I went for ma lunch.'

Gently said quietly, 'Then you better hadn't say other. And now, I am sure you will have raised a thirst.'

'Aye – I'm fair parched!'

'And one word more.' Gently placed his finger to his lips. Then he touched Collins on the shoulder and nodded back towards the mill.

There, a customer was waiting, and had to be dealt with before Collins could bolt his door again. It intrigued Gently to notice how quickly the antique dealer could conquer his agitation and assume his customary professional manner. The customer was American. He was hunting netsukes. From a cabinet, Collins produced an alluring trayful. He produced others from his safe and laid them out preciously on a display-table. It took time, but the result was worth it, and a surprising bundle of notes changed hands. Collins saw his profitable customer to the door and returned with the notes still in his grasp. Then he shoved them in the safe.

'As though any of this matters – now!'

He led Gently to the office-workshop, which still reeked of french polish, and threw himself down on a chair.

'What the devil am I going to do?'

Gently also sat. He said, 'There's one thing you would be well advised not to do, and that's to offer bribes to inconvenient witnesses.'

'But I wasn't going to bribe him!'

132

'I think he read it that way. And he wasn't disinclined to accept. But I'm afraid you will have to live with it – the testimony is that your car was available.'

'But I didn't know that.'

'So you say.'

'I just didn't. Won't anyone believe me?'

Gently said, 'Let's get to that phone call. I take it there was no clue as to where Angus was phoning from?'

Collins shook his head. 'It sounded close, as though it might have come from the box down the street. But you can't tell. I've had calls from abroad that sounded as though they came from the next room.'

'But it was from a box.'

'Oh yes.'

'Did he need to feed in extra coins?'

'No.' Collins stared. 'It would have to be somewhere close, wouldn't it?'

'May I use your phone?'

Gently rang the police station and passed on the information: probably too late for any positive result, but it offered the search a point of reference. He hung up. Collins was still staring.

'He – he could be just round the corner, couldn't he?'

'He would have to hide his car.'

'But there are lots of places! He might even have dumped it in the loch.'

'And he was seriously threatening you?'

'Yes, he was. He swore he was innocent, so it had to be me. He pretends to believe I was after his wife, and that when she wouldn't listen to me, I strangled her.'

'And – Fowler?'

'Because Fowler had recognized me, and was going to tell the police. Oh, he had it all pat! It's the story he means to tell when you pick him up.'

'And which is quite ridiculous?'

'You know it is!'

'Unfortunately, it could fit the facts.'

'But you wouldn't – you can't believe that.' Now the fear in Collins' eyes was very real. 'You can't mean this.'

Gently shrugged. 'If Angus should be innocent, it is a case

133

we would have to look at. And I might be obliged to record my impression that you were willing to suborn a witness.'

'But he isn't innocent!'

'We don't know that.'

'And last night – when he thought he was getting away with it!'

Gently said, 'All I can testify about last night is that you were late returning home, and that I found you in a very emotional condition.'

'But that's as good as to say –'

'Those are the facts.'

'I don't believe this,' Collins said. 'I can't! I thought you were friends, you and Mrs Gently, and yet all the time you seem out to trap me. Is that the idea?'

Gently fingered the phone. He said, 'Look at it for a moment from the police point of view! All our information points to your being in the glen, however vehemently you deny it. You were there, you had opportunity, you may or may not have had an adequate motive. And you were twice seen by Fowler who, during the altercation with Angus, was facing the road at a distance of a few yards. Whether Fowler was acquainted with you or not, he could still have described the car and the driver, and it seems clear from the message he left at The Clachan that he regarded that as significant information.'

'But none of this is true!'

'Just a moment! Now we come to last night. By your own admission you were passing in the street and saw Fowler waiting to use the phone-box.'

'I didn't know it was him!'

'We have independent testimony that Fowler was present there at exactly that time, and that shortly afterwards a tallish man in dark clothing was seen hurrying down the track towards the river. There, some while later, Fowler was battered to death and his body cast into the stream, and his killer escaped unobserved, though the disturbance was heard and the time noted by a witness.'

'But it was Angus – and then he came after me!'

'We have only your word that he made that visit.'

'But he did – and I told you all about it!'

Gently shook his head. 'It rests solely on your word. All I can testify for certain is that I found you in a highly nervous state, and that, to the best of my observation, you were expecting to be arrested. To that I would have to add my impression of your recent application to the garage-attendant. And that is the case you may have to face if Angus should be able to demonstrate his innocence.'

'But . . . he can't. How can he!'

Gently said, 'The case against him at the moment is entirely circumstantial.'

'No. He did it!'

Gently stroked the phone. He said, 'Of course, additional evidence may yet come to hand.'

'Additional evidence?'

'Fresh testimony. Of how matters stood up the glen.'

'Up . . . the glen?'

Gently said nothing: stared into the antique dealer's frightened eyes.

'But . . . this is blackmail!'

Gently said nothing.

'I can't – I won't! It's a trap!'

Gently shrugged.

'Oh lord!' Collins wailed. 'There must be some way out but this. I've got to tell lies?'

Gently stared at him.

'But then – you'd pull me in at once!'

'It is entirely up to you, Mr Collins.'

Collins groaned and hugged his head.

'How – how much would I have to tell?'

Gently had got up and gone to stare through the window. There, below, beneath the green gloom of sycamores, the waters rushed by the rocks of the jackdaws' island. The room was on the side of the mill furthest from the parking and was penetrated by the sound of the water. In there, it was credible that one might not hear the sound of a car being parked outside.

'I know the place of course. I've often been up there. But . . .'

Gently said, 'I don't think I have to prompt you.'

135

'No! But exactly what . . .?'

Gently shook his head, and sat himself again.

'I mean – if I was there! – I'd have seen them rowing, and of course I wouldn't have wanted to stop. But that wouldn't be enough, would it? You know all about that already . . .'

Gently picked up a figurine that lay on the desk and tilted it, to examine the mark.

'I'd have had to turn the car . . .' Collins was hugging himself. 'Of course they would see me – especially Fowler! And then I must have seen . . . though, if she'd been in hiding . . . yet I suppose. When I turned the car . . .'

Gently said, 'Where were the two men when you saw them?'

'Where . . .? I didn't specially notice!'

'And their cars. Where were they parked?'

'Well, at the roadside . . . there's a bit of a bay.'

'Both together.'

'Yes.'

'And the men. Weren't they over by the stream?'

'Yes, I suppose . . .'

'Near that broken-down willow?'

'Yes . . . they were over there.'

Gently sighed, and replaced the figurine. He said, 'How much for a piece of Staffordshire like that? My sister has a birthday shortly, and something of this sort could be the answer.'

'But that isn't –' Collins began, then he stopped. He sat goggling at Gently. 'You don't believe me, do you?'

'It isn't Worcester,' Gently said. 'I know Worcester.'

'Oh my God!' Collins said. 'Now I don't know where I am. Are you going to arrest me?'

'Could it be Doulton?'

'Oh, please!' Collins said. 'For God's sake tell me where I stand. A moment ago I was almost believing . . . and now all you can talk about is china!'

Gently said, 'What else is there to talk about? It couldn't have been you up the glen on Monday. And if you weren't, then you had no motive for pursuing and silencing Fowler.'

'You mean that all you were saying – ?'

'We are back with the doctor. And a Volvo that may always have been a red herring.'

136

'And it's . . . all right?'

'Perhaps you'll tell me it's Dresden. But I do know enough not to fall for that.'

Collins sank back in his chair with a groan. Sweat had gathered on his creased brow. He stared at Gently, still unbelieving a dazed look in the blue eyes. Then he started up again.

'But Inspector Blayne! He will still be thinking – ?'

Gently shook his head. 'Inspector Blayne will remain preoccupied with the doctor.'

'He will take your word?'

Gently shrugged. 'At the moment the doctor is our first priority. The car has been a problem, but it may be that we can eliminate it now.'

'Because . . . it wasn't mine.'

Gently nodded.

'But the doctor. He's still on the loose!'

'Perhaps it won't be for long.'

Collins' head drooped. 'He's really got it in for me,' he said. 'I'm to be his scapegoat. You should have heard him. Perhaps I should be asking for police protection.'

Gently thought about it, but shook his head. Collins sat staring at the figurine. Then the phone went. Collins snatched at it. He listened, then tremblingly handed it to Gently. Gently took it. He said:

'Hullo?'

But after a moment, the phone went dead.

'And you're thinkin' it was him again,' Blayne said musingly. 'That he's really tryin' to put some pressure on that whey-faced chiel? But ach! How could he think we would swallow it, and him so dooms deep in the business himself?'

Collins had been and Collins had gone: after undergoing a second grilling, from the sceptical Scot. He had perhaps done right to be fearful of the suspicions that Blayne might entertain. Gently could throw doubt on Collins' presence in the glen, but in the matter of Fowler there could be no question: Collins had seen Fowler, he had had opportunity, and was found in an emotional state shortly afterwards. Because of harassment by the doctor? Ach, but that could be just a tale! And the same with the phone call – it could be a wee sleight to keep the polis looking somewhere else. By the time he was finally dismissed poor Collins was well-nigh in despair, and seemed amazed to be shown the police station door instead of being led to a cell.

'It is still circumstantial,' Gently said. 'As yet we have nothing material against Angus. It rests purely on motive, opportunity and his recent behaviour. I suppose nothing useful has come in from forensic?'

Blayne shook his head. 'You cannot expect it. There'll be no prints on a chunk o' granite. And the only clear footprint on the bank is one matchin' the trainers the laddie was wearin'.'

'There's some useful undergrowth down there.'

'Aye, and the lads have been through it with a comb. They came up with a scrap of woo' from a bramble, but –' Blayne pulled a face – 'it matched a rent in my own good trews.'

'No other witnesses?'

'Na. We're stuck with Scruffy Jock still. I'm tryin' to trace the lady Collins says was in the phone-box, but like as not she was a visitor just passin' through.'

'And of course – no news yet of the doctor?'

'Not a scrap. He's sittin' tight somewhere.'

'Somewhere near a phone-box.'

Blayne nodded. 'If we're for believin' the loon who was just in here.'

'I think I believe him,' Gently said. 'And my guess is it can't be so far away. Angus had very little margin when he left here, and he knew the hunt would be up the moment you missed him.'

He related his conversation with the garage-attendant. Blayne listened with wary eyes.

'Ach, the long-haired loon! But he's right so far. There are no lock-up garages in the town.'

'Would you know of any empty premises?'

'I could not say, off the top of my head. But would the doctor know of them, either?'

'He had several days here. To spy out the land.'

'Aye . . . so he had.' Blayne's eyes were even narrower. 'And we've had no smell o' him round about. And fules we would look if the cunnin' chiel were lodged here, right under our noses. Purdy!' he called. The sharp-faced sergeant presented himself at the office door. 'Purdy, you'll just be sortin' out any empty properties they may have around the town.'

'Empty properties, sir . . .?'

'Aye, you loon! Houses with garages and the like. Check if the local laddies can tell us – and give the local agents a call. And Purdy.'

'Yes, sir?'

'Just report back. I don't want you bangin' on any doors.'

Purdy departed promptly. Blayne rubbed his hands and looked at Gently. Gently said:

'One other move. It might be worthwhile to put a tap on Collins' phone.'

'Ach, I should have thought of it!' Blayne said. 'Though the chiel may be cautious after gettin' you at the mill. But we'll do it. I'm takin' no chances. I want that doctor sittin' here. And should you have any other wee wrinkles, spit them out, man. I'm here to listen.'

But Gently had no more to suggest. He sat by while Blayne arranged for the tap, then rose to leave. Blayne accompanied him to the door and stood a moment regarding the peaceful street. He said:

'When we take him, you'll be for sittin' in?'

'Provided my sister gives permission,' Gently said.

'Ach, I keep forgettin' you're here on holiday, man!' Blayne said. 'And here I'm takin' your time up still. I'm no' in her bad books?'

'Bridget understands.'

Blayne sighed, and stared at the lengthening shadows in the street. 'It's a sair business,' he said. 'And in a bonnie place. I hope it may not sour your impressions o' Leary.'

Gently lit his pipe, and left. Once more, he paused at the bridge. Would those two tragedies haunt his memory of the falls, the island, the comfortable Clachan? He hoped not. The sun was leaning on the hill, the pines on the island were shadowy. Children were being called from the rocks. And the parking by the mill was empty of Volvos. He went his way.

'You're late,' Bridget said. 'I've had to keep your meal warm under the grill. Don't blame me if it's dried up. Did they have to send to Glasgow for that tobacco?'

Gabrielle met him with a look of inquiry. But Gently merely shrugged, and sat down to his meal.

11

No one had very much to say that evening, as the long twilight slipped away. It was as though the subject of the tragedies had become suddenly taboo, to be replaced by an aching vacuum. Gently helped Gabrielle with the dishes. Bridget sat knitting with a pattern before her. Even the usually cheerful Geoffrey was content to stare languidly at a sub-standard TV programme. Outside the jackdaws had settled down and a mist had claimed the ben and its supporting hills, as it had done the evening before. It was the same hour: and that perhaps was present in all their minds. When the dishes were done, Gently and Gabrielle returned to the lounge and joined Geoffrey in hopefully scanning the TV, but no amount of switching between channels produced a faintly acceptable offering. At last Geoffrey threw down the control box.

'What's the use of hanging around here?' he said. 'Come on, Bridgie, that sweater will wait. Let's go and drown our sorrows at The Clachan.'

'If we do, someone's bound to grab George,' Bridget said. 'And there will be only one subject of conversation.'

'Well, we'll grab him straight back,' Geoffrey said. 'And we don't have to listen if we don't want to.'

'That landlord is bound to descend on us.'

'So freeze him off with one of your stares.'

'Oh, please yes, let us go,' Gabrielle said. 'It is better we do not sit about here.'

So Bridget buried her needles in her ball of wool and Geoffrey switched off the TV, and they set out, a little grimly in Bridget's case, to saunter across to The Clachan. But it turned out better

141

than she had supposed. At this hour few of the outside tables were occupied, while Geoffrey, who had been dispatched to the bar for the drinks, succeeded in avoiding Menzies' eye. They chose a table as remote from the bar as possible, and settled down to watch the falls, the strollers and the occasional passing car. Gently had glanced round the tables, half-expecting to find Collins there, but the only person he recognized was Frazer, the dapper boss of Kinleary Motors. Frazer had given him an interested nod, but happily had not sought to accost him. So they drank unmolested, and even Bridget began to relax.

'Tomorrow, we could make that trip to Fort William.' She eyed her brother. 'Provided George can tear himself away.'

'Can you?' Geoffrey grinned. 'After all, it's only a matter now of nabbing the doctor. Routine, don't you call it?'

'Ha, yes,' Gabrielle said. 'Because now it is certain that poor Mr Collins is innocent. And it will be good to get away a little, to see some other new places.'

'George,' Bridget said.

Gently drank some bitter. 'It may not be quite so straightforward,' he said.

'But can there be any doubt left?' Bridget said. 'Even I have to agree that the doctor is the man they want.'

'And that's saying something!' Geoffrey grinned. 'Because Bridget has always stood up for the doctor. And dear old Blayne can't be having many doubts. Short of homicidal maniacs, it stays with the doctor.'

'George,' Bridget said.

Gently drank some more. 'You don't have to stay around here,' he said.

'That means you won't come?'

He shook his head. 'But I would prefer to be present when they talk to Angus.'

Geoffrey stared at him keenly. 'You know something,' he said.

'Nothing that Blayne doesn't know,' Gently said. 'Just that there may be some angles to the business, points that can't be cleared up till we talk to the man.'

'But can't Blayne clear them up?'

'Probably.'

'Then in your case it's just professional curiosity.'

'Of course it is,' Bridget said. 'George simply wants to be in at the kill. It's always the same with him. He has to dot every i and cross every t.'

'But perhaps . . . just this time?' Gabrielle said wistfully.

Gently stared at the falls, and drank again. What was it that still troubled him about this affair, except that still it was resting on circumstantiality?

'Come on, old man,' Geoffrey said. 'You can always talk to the doctor afterwards – just suppose they nab him while we're away!'

'Yes, you can do that,' Gabrielle said eagerly. 'I am sure the good Blayne will not object.'

Gently shrugged. 'Very well, then,' he said.

'Tomorrow – we shall go to this Fort William?'

'Yes. Tomorrow.'

'Oh my dear, you are kind!'

'Perhaps now we can make arrangements,' Bridget said tartly.

Geoffrey fetched fresh drinks, and they talked on, but now only of routes, times and arrangements for meals. Gently listened to them silently, his eyes on the falls, the misted hill. Was it the character of the man that was bothering him, some discrepancy between the actor and the deeds? Yet he recognized violence as an element in the doctor, and violence he had employed in his first encounter with Fowler. Enough violence . . . homicidal violence? The fearful Collins had had little doubt. Unless he agreed to be the doctor's scapegoat he was liable to become the third victim. But . . . could the doctor have credibly expected Collins to confess, aware as he must be of the antique dealer's innocence – if those were the circumstances, what possible prospect of success could he entertain? Was it merely to bolster his own aspect of innocence that he had behaved as he did?

'Oh no,' Bridget said. 'Oh no!'

Gently's attention switched suddenly. Scruffy Jock had just crossed the bridge, had seen them, and was heading for their table. He caught the eye of his boss and rocked his shoulders apologetically, but continued towards where they sat, a disreputable figure in oil-stained jeans.

143

'Yes?' Bridget snapped.

'If I could have a word, noo –'

'At the moment we have no need of petrol.'

'Ach, just a word wi' this gentleman, if he doesna mind!'

Bridget glared at Gently. 'So there he sits.'

'But – a word, if he wull, in private . . .'

'Oh, my goodness!' Bridget said. 'Who would go on holiday with such a brother?'

Gently rose. He beckoned the garageman aside. He led him to stand by the parapet of the bridge. He said:

'Now!'

Scruffy Jock rocked himself. 'It's aboot whit we were talkin' of earlier –'

'About hiding cars?'

'Aye. An' I thought I'd take a wee peek around.'

'And?'

'Weel . . . you ken that rough ground, doon by the brig at the other end? It's just across from the chiel Collins' hoose, an' no' many steps fra the turnpike. Weel, I'm castin' my een in there. An' I'm seein' the rump end o' a grey Mercedes.'

Gently stared at him. 'Wait here.' He hastened back to the others at the table. 'I'm sorry,' he said. 'But something has come up. I promise I'll be back as soon as I'm able.'

Bridget fixed him with her eye. 'George,' she said, 'it's Fort William tomorrow. Is that quite understood?'

'Understood.'

'Oh please, do not be late!' Gabrielle said.

Gently ducked his head. And departed.

'Did you see the doctor?'

'Ach, no! There's just his car, sittin' there in the bushes.'

'Was Collins at home?'

'I canna just say. I cam' awa' straight to bring you the news.'

They were hastening across the bridge, now almost forsaken by the strollers. Dusk had fallen, and lights were shimmering a little in the mist, down the street. They turned the corner and hurried on.

'Why did you not report straight to the police?'

144

'Ach, you ken how it is!' His head twisted. 'I'm no' just frien's wi' the polis round here.'

'Why is that?'

'Why? Am I no' a puir mannie wha lives in a van? They would have me oot o' that, you ken, an' the council have had words wi' Mr Mackenzie. But the boss, he's a decent laddie, he willna listen to their blethers.'

'Well, you'll be reporting to the police now.'

'Aye. But wi' a mannie like you at ma shoulder.'

They arrived at the police station. Blayne had left, but Purdy had remained i/c. When he heard what Scruffy Jock had to tell he made a quick call through to Balmagussie. Then the patrols were swiftly alerted and a pair of uniform men detailed. In two cars they set out from the police station, with Scruffy Jock riding behind Purdy and Gently. Purdy screwed his head round.

'And you're sure it's the right car?'

'Oh aye. It couldna have been any other.'

'You'd just better be right!' Purdy said.

Quickly they came to the glen turn-off, parked and tumbled out of the cars. Scruffy Jock led them through the opening to the strath and behind a screen of birch and hazel. Then he stood back.

'Now be callin' me a liar!'

Driven in among the bushes, the grey Mercedes stood parked there. Purdy pulled out his notebook and checked the registration, then tried the doors and felt the bonnet.

'It's still warm, sir!' He turned on Scruffy Jock. 'Just when do you say you spotted this car?'

'Ach, it canna be much more than half an hour. I cam' straight awa' up to find the Superintendent.'

'And you did not see the driver?'

'Na, I'm tellin' you!'

'Man, you must have gone near to bumpin' into him!'

'Na, there was no one. It was like it is now, no' a soul aboot, no' here or in the road.'

Purdy stared keenly at Scruffy Jock. Gently said:

'The car is missing from Collins' drive.'

'He could be at the mill, sir.'

145

Gently shook his head. 'When we passed it, his car wasn't there either.'

'You're sayin' – ?' Purdy's eyes grew large. 'Oh my Gawd, let's get over there! You men, never mind the car, just follow me to yon house!'

'You're not wantin' me still?' Scruffy Jock said.

'Hang about or clear off – I'll know where to find you!'

The portents were not good. Not only was the Volvo missing from the drive. Among its shrubberies the tall house stood silent with not a glimmer of light from any of its windows. Purdy rang the bell. Chimes sounded hollowly. He rang again. There was no reply. On the gravel of the drive, fresh tyre-marks suggested that a car might recently have departed from thence.

'Ach, the devil! What are we goin' to find inside?'

'Better check the garden.'

'Fetch torches, you men!'

Torches were fetched from the cars. Two patrol cars arrived, and their crews were at once added to the strength of the searchers. Lights flickered in the shrubberies, down the walled garden, in a shed and a greenhouse at the bottom.

'Nothing here, sir.'

'We'll have to go in!'

'First,' Gently said, 'put out a call for the Volvo.'

'Ach, yes!'

Purdy himself went to do it, and returned with a jangling ring of keys in his hand.

'One of you stand by the kitchen door, and the rest of you spread out round the house!'

The disposition was made. Purdy advanced to the front door.

'Just one more try,' Gently said. He pressed the bell, and then, when there was no answer, called, 'Collins – Angus. We are the police. If you are in there, you had best come out.' But no sound came from the darkened house, and Gently motioned Purdy to continue. The lock conceded. The door opened. This time, no chain was barring the way.

'Two of you come with us, and one of you stand guard on the door.'

Purdy found the switch that lit the hall and the four of them marched in.

146

'You two upstairs.'

Working together, he and Gently threw open the doors of the rooms below, rooms stuffed with furniture, books, china and other gear of Collins' trade. All appeared to be in order, with no obvious signs of recent violence. In the kitchen crockery was stacked to dry on the draining-board and a dishcloth folded and draped over the sink. Gently felt the electric kettle: it was not quite cold, but probably hadn't been in use since Collins' evening meal.

'Any sign o' life up there?'

'No sir . . . but we havena been in the loft!'

'Ach, forget the loft!'

'Then that's the lot, sir. Nothin' up here.'

'Nothin' . . .'

Purdy stared fretfully at the cabinets and book-cases in the hall. That house was too tidy! For all one could read there, Collins had simply locked up and departed on his lawful occasions. And yet, across the road . . .

'He must have come here, sir. He would not have driven this way for the sake o' his health.'

'Was that spot across the road checked earlier?'

'Aye. We had a car right down the glen.' Purdy paused. 'You could not be thinkin' now . . . rememberin' his auld tricks with a body . . .?'

Gently shrugged: yes, it was possible. And the river, the loch beckoned. But if Collins had been attacked it hadn't been in that undisturbed house.

'Check outside for signs of a struggle.'

Purdy hastily gathered his men. With torches they inspected the gravel in the drive, where the returning antique dealer might most likely have been ambushed. Then the check extended to the lawn, the flower-beds and, less hopefully, the grounds at the rear, but without success. If Collins had been attacked, then the odds were it had been somewhere off the premises.

'Could he have throttled him in the car, sir?'

'He would have needed to force his way into it.'

Purdy stared at the tyre-marks in the gravel, but nowhere were there signs of violent, thrusting feet.

'If the chiel had conned his way in . . .'

'Collins was well aware of his danger.'

'If he'd had a gun, now . . .'

But Gently shook his head. That Angus was provided with a gun was not very likely.

'Ach, I don't know, sir!' Purdy kept staring. 'It's almost as though they were in this together – in cahoots, the pair of them – for all we're turnin' up here. Would that just be possible?'

'Highly improbable.'

'But it would square with what's here, sir. The doctor's car across the road, and nothin' about the premises suggestin' foul play.'

'It would require Collins to have been a superlative actor.'

'I would not quite put it past the loon. And the doctor, he's no' short of cash, he could be offerin' a tidy hand-out.'

'But to do what?'

'Ach, to see him clear! To whisk him away out o' our ken. He's a marked man, drivin' his Mercedes, but no' huddled under rugs in the back of an estate.'

Gently considered it, but shook his head again. 'It would need to be someone other than Collins! The bribe doesn't exist that would persuade him to put himself in the hands of the doctor.'

'So where is that leavin' us?'

'Where we were before.'

'With a body to look for?'

Gently shrugged. 'As of now, a few inquiries among the neighbours here. Then a search along the river and the shores of the loch.'

'And – for one green Volvo estate.'

Gently nodded. 'And its driver.'

'Right, then,' Purdy said. 'Gather round, you men!'

But before he could brief them there came an interruption. The lights of a car appeared from up the glen, drew closer, hesitated, then signalled a turn.

'Oh, my gosh . . .!'

The car entered the drive. It stopped, cut its engine and lights. It was a green Volvo estate. And out of it climbed a terrified Collins.

* * *

148

'What – this isn't – you can't be arresting me!'

Collins shrank fearfully against the Volvo. And he had some reason for his apprehension: Purdy was stalking menacingly towards him.

'You can't – you can't –'

'So what have you done with him?'

'Done with him?'

'Aye, that murtherin' doctor!'

'But –'

'You've hidden him, haven't you? Up the glen. You've found some hole there to stash him in.'

'But – this is impossible!'

'You're tellin' me that – when yon's his car tucked away in the bushes? Ach, no, we were not born yesterday! So now we'll be hearin' where you left him, Mr Collins.'

'But I repeat –'

'Where's the doctor?'

'I don't know where he is!'

'And you'll be tellin' me next you have not seen him?'

'No, I haven't!'

'Ach, and do you want me to be shakin' it out o' you?'

'Hold on!' Gently advanced and laid a hand on Purdy's arm. For a moment Purdy remained poised threateningly, then he fell back to make way for Gently.

'But you hear him denyin' it!'

'It may be true.'

'Ach, with the car parked outside his gate?'

'All the same!' Gently turned to Collins. 'Perhaps you had better tell us where you've been this evening.'

The trembling Collins stared at Gently. 'I – I've been visiting Tosh McDermid! I –'

'You have spent the evening with him?'

'Yes! I wanted to be out of reach of the phone.'

'All the evening?'

'Yes – since tea! I didn't want any more of those threatening calls. Then there was a deal we had on with his pictures, the ones left over from the exhibition.'

'And at no time have you set eyes on Angus?'

'No, But –' Collins' eyes were big – 'what is all this about?'

149

Gently said, 'I'm afraid this may alarm you. At some time this evening Dr Angus was in the neighbourhood. We received a report of his car being seen here, a report which we naturally treated with urgency. The absence of yourself and your car seemed ominous and we felt it necessary to enter your house.'

'But . . . why?'

'We found his car parked across the road, and yours was absent. It suggested certain conclusions.'

'Oh God! And you thought –'

'It doesn't matter now.'

'But you searched the house.'

'Just a routine precaution.'

Collins grabbed at the car. 'And he's still around here – you haven't found him?'

'We know now he is in the area. And that he is on foot.'

'And after me!'

'If that was his intention, he has no prospect of carrying it out now.'

Collins would have collapsed, but Purdy caught him, and with the help of a uniform man he was carted into the house. There he was laid out on a settee while some foraging set him up with a snifter of brandy. Purdy drew Gently aside.

'This McDermid, sir –'

'He's a painter. He lives in the first cottage up the glen.'

'Should we not be givin' him a visit, then?'

After a moment, Gently nodded. Purdy briefed two of the men, and they departed up the glen. But . . . if Collins was acting a part! Gently stared at the woeful antique dealer, and shrugged.

'Keep a man stationed under cover by the car, and get those neighbourhood inquiries under way. And send a man round to the hotel. Someone may have seen the car turn in here.'

Purdy said, 'That car is still warm, sir. I cannot think how Jock Mackay missed seein' the doctor.'

'The doctor may have seen him first.'

'Aye. But I'm vexed now I let the man go. He's no' so well thought of in Leary, and I would not put it past him to be playin' his own game.'

'He did report the car.'

150

'But no' direct to us, sir. And that would give the doctor a few more minutes.'

'He needn't have made a report at all.'

But Purdy shook his head. 'It's still a wee queer to me.'

He left to put the inquiries in train, and Gently took a chair by the demoralized Collins. The brandy had returned a trace of colour to his always-pallid cheeks, but he was still gazing blankly with terrified eyes.

'He – he meant to kill me. You know that!'

'We cannot be certain of his intentions.'

'But what else could they be? He's running amuck. It doesn't matter now how many he kills!'

'He may still have hoped to force a confession.'

'But how could he, when he knew I was innocent?'

'If he was convinced it was you who were up the glen –'

'But I wasn't – I wasn't – I wasn't!'

'Still . . . if he had thought so?'

Collins's eyes burned into his. 'You know it wasn't me. You know it.'

'Yet so easily it could have been.'

'I don't care! How could he have imagined that I would confess?'

Gently said, 'There could be just one reason. If it was someone else who strangled Angus's wife.'

'Someone else – ?' Shock was in his eyes. 'But – how could it have been someone else?'

'It would explain his behaviour towards yourself.'

'But you can't think – you can't believe!'

'I am trying to understand the doctor's motives.'

Collins shuddered. He threw back the brandy. The glass was shaking in his hand. He stared at it, stared at Gently. He gave a groan that was half a sob.

'It had to be him . . . you're just saying this! You know it wasn't me who was up the glen.'

'But . . . if the doctor had thought so?'

'He's mad – mad. His brain is gone. He was just trying it on.'

'But if by chance he was innocent?'

'No!'

151

'It might explain this visit tonight.'

'No, he came to kill me. That was what you thought. That was why you broke in here . . . looking for my corpse!'

Gently shrugged. 'It might yet have been his motive.'

'It doesn't matter. He came to kill me!'

'On the phone, is that what he threatened?'

But Collins merely groaned, 'I want police protection!'

Purdy hurried back. He said, 'We've got a witness who saw the car drive in, sir! He thought it might be a courting couple, but then he sees a man come slopin' away.'

'He saw the doctor?'

'I've got him here, sir. He's a neighbour from down the road.'

An elderly man: his name was Miller; he'd been drawing his window-curtains when he saw the car arrive. It had cut its lights and driven on to the strath without signalling the turn, and Miller had paused at the window a moment, brooding on the immorality of the younger generation. Then he had seen a man emerge from the opening and stare hard towards Collins' house, before, after a moment's hesitation, setting off in the direction of the bridge.

'Could you describe him?'

'Now you're askin'! This was in the gloamin', you understand. But he was no' a short man, and he was dressed sober, and I wouldna say he was just a youngster.'

'Can you give the time?'

'Aye. It was just startin' the ten o'clock news.'

'You saw no one else?'

'Na, why would I? I drew the curtains and settled down.'

'And you are sure of the direction he took?'

'Aye, I'm tellin' you. Towards the bridge.'

Gently said to Purdy, 'Send another man along to make inquiries around the hotel, and one up the road towards town. He may be still somewhere in the area.'

'No' if he's got his marbles,' Purdy said, and he went to convey the orders. But at just that moment a car drew up, and an excited Blayne charged on to the scene. He grabbed hold of Purdy.

'Have we got him, then? Is the slippery devil inside?'

152

'No' just yet,' Purdy said. 'But we're on the trail, sir. It cannot be so very long now.'

'Ach, and here's himself!' Blayne exclaimed, catching sight of Gently. 'I kent you'd be in at the kill, man. And the chiel Collins the bait an a' – man, it's workin' out just fine!'

Collins wailed, 'I demand protection! That man came here for only one purpose.'

'And what protection are you needin', man,' Blayne leered, 'with half the constabulary runnin' in and out here?'

'But he means to kill me!'

'Aye, maybe. And like that's just been the loon's undoing. So do not be lookin' so whey-faced, my mannie, you'll no' become a patient of Dr Angus's.'

Gently gave him a brief résumé and Blayne listened with a lively eye. He said:

'Ach, and it could not have been in better hands, man. Listenin' to you is an education. And you'll be for hangin' on here a wee while, just to see the face o' that devil?'

Gently shook his head. 'You're in charge now.'

'Aweel, then I'll find you a car,' Blayne said.

Gently looked at his watch. 'I'll walk,' he said. 'By now The Clachan will be closed anyway.'

He left Blayne with the miserable Collins. The glen road was unlit, and stars sparkled above it. Just for a moment he remained staring at the opening beyond which the grey Mercedes lay ensconced in its bushes, then he turned back to look at the green Volvo that stood in the drive of the antique dealer's house.

12

'Any luck?'

'No' this way, sir.'

Gently had turned into the road leading back to the town. It too was ill-lit, and trees cast deep shadow on the side bordering the head of the loch. On the other side was a scattering of houses, some large and set in shrubby gardens. At the gate of one of these a uniform man had been conversing with the resident. Then he had turned away, to recommence slowly patrolling the deserted road.

'Weren't you one of those sent to check with McDermid?'

'Aye, I was, sir. It needed but a word.'

'And Collins had been there, as he said?'

'Just the way he said, sir. He'd been there since seven.' The man paused. 'Though it was not just about paintings, so I gathered from Mr McDermid. He was wantin' him to think again about seein' him that way on the Monday.'

'To change his testimony.'

'Aye. But Mr McDermid said he couldna. And he was for persuadin' Collins to come out with it, and to set himself straight with us.'

'He was convinced he had seen him?'

'Aye. But he could not persuade Collins.'

Gently nodded. 'Thank you.' He left the man to his patrolling. Higher up, the man who the constable had been talking to still lingered at his gate. Gently approached him. He had recognized him as Frazer from the garage. As he drew level, Frazer said:

'So what's it all about then, if a body may ask?'

Gently said, 'How long have you been back here?'

154

'Ach, yon constable was asking me that! I hung on at The Clachan till closing – I got on to a darts game in the bar.'

'And you met no one on your way here?'

'No' but some visitors turning out of the Castle Hotel. But what's it about? I saw you talking to Scruffy, and carting him off. He's no' in trouble, is he?'

Gently regarded him. Frazer's eyes were anxious in the glint of a street-light.

'What do we know about him – this rather unusual employee of yours?'

'Ach, just nothing! He's an honest mannie.'

'But one not above an occasional lie?'

'He's had his troubles, you ken, poor old Scruffy –'

'But he might lie – if it served his interests?'

'Oh dear!' Frazer dropped his gaze. 'I warned the loon that this might happen. I'm telling you, I pleaded with him to come clean, but no, he wouldna. He does not trust the polis. And now – you're on to him?'

Gently said nothing.

'Man, you cannot be too hard. It was just to keep himself clear of trouble – you ken, he's had dealings with the polis before.'

Gently said, 'What dealings?'

'Ach, nothing serious. A wee matter of being cotched with drugs, he once told me. That was long since, but it made the loon wary. And he could not tell you anything you didna know.'

'He couldn't?'

Frazer shook his neat head. 'You kent already what he saw up the glen. Just the doctor and the boy-friend having it out, and the lady nowhere to be seen.'

Gently stared very hard. 'He saw that?'

'He was but giving the car a test run. And he kent I spotted him bringing the car back, and we had it out on our own in the office.' Frazer ventured a wink. 'And I backed the loon up – there could not be so much harm in it! But not before I'd begged him to make a clean breast. You'll be for giving me the credit for that.'

Gently was silent for several moments. He looked at Frazer, Frazer looked at him. At last Gently said:

155

'I'll repeat my question. What do we know about Jock Mackay?'

'Man, there's no harm in him – none at all!'

'How long has he been an employee of yours?'

Frazer wrinkled his brow. 'It must be eight or nine years. And I ken no dishonesty in him, that's straight. He would not touch a penny that wasna his own.'

'How did you come to take him on?'

'How did I?' A smirk showed on Frazer's face. 'At first it was to pay for a bust exhaust, and then it carried on from there.'

'A bust exhaust . . . .?'

'Aye. He pulled in here one afternoon. His old van was sounding like a salvo of artillery, and there was not a cupful left in the tank. He couldna go on, so I let him stay till I could get a replacement from Glasgow. And he had no more brass than he had petrol. I was short of staff. I put him on the pumps.'

'And he's stayed ever since?'

Frazer nodded. 'And I cannot say I have regretted it. His old van is out of the way there, and it's no' bad thing to have him round the place.'

'Has he ever spoken of his past?'

'Just a hint of his trouble, and telling a few tales of his time on the road. He likes his dram, but he does not seek company. Jock is a loner, first and last.'

'And – he was up the glen on Monday.'

'Man, now you ken it, he'll tell you all he knows! But you must not blame the auld devil too much. He's had his problems, has Jock Mackay.'

Gently hesitated, then shrugged and bid the garage-owner good-night. He strode on. It was near midnight, and not a soul was stirring in the town's narrow street. The police station had lights and one car stood on the parking. Drawing abreast of it, he slackened pace, but after a moment hastened on. He came to the garage. It was dark, except for a faint glow in the corner of the yard. Without checking, he strode across to it and knocked on the door of the van. The door opened suddenly.

'Aye – so it's you!'

Scruffy Jock stared past him: at the yard, at the empty street.

'You were expecting someone?'

'No' just expectin' – unless the chiel Purdy took a notion to come round.'

'Then may I come in?'

'Weel, it's past my bedtime . . .'

'This shouldn't take very long.'

The brown eyes peered through the lank, shaggy hair, and the garageman's solid body blocked the narrow doorway. He said, 'If it's no' just a life-and-death matter, could it no' wait till the morrow morn?'

'It may well be a life-and-death matter.'

'Weel . . . in that case . . .' He stood back from the door.

At night, with curtains drawn, the van had a cocoon-like feel, an impression heightened by the fumes given off by the hurricane-lamp that lighted it. By the door, on one side, was a cooking-galley, on the other the door of a toilet compartment. Then there were two bunks and two sideboard-cupboards and a cavernous recess above the driver's cockpit, the latter apparently containing a double-berth, but beyond the range of the lamp's limited illumination. A folding table occupied much of the floor space. A sleeping-bag lay rolled on one of the bunks.

'Sit you down, then . . .'

Scruffy Jock had preceded Gently into the van. Now he tucked his large body in beside the table with the deftness of long familiarity. Gently squeezed in just clear of the table. He gave a stare to the recess and to the curtained-off cockpit. Then, quite casually, he picked up the hurricane and raised it until its light fell in the former.

'Ach, we're alone here – there's just the two o' us!'

Silently, Gently replaced the lamp. He regarded the bristly face that stared at him across the table. He said:

'I've just been having a few words with your boss.'

'Wi' – Mr Frazer?'

Gently nodded.

'An' – whit's he been sayin'?'

'I think you can guess.'

'Ach, but he wouldna!'

Gently said nothing.

157

'Oh, ma gosh!' Scruffy Jock swung his hair. 'But I wasna meanin' any harm, you ken. It was just I didna want any part o' it – you ken weel the polis an' I are no' friendly.'

'A small matter of drugs?'

'He shouldna have said so! But aye, if you like, I have ma reasons.'

'And it didn't trouble you that we might suspect Collins?'

'Ach, how was I to ken he'd been up wi' the lady?'

'Or that you would be wasting a great deal of police time?'

'Na, I didna think they'd be makin' such a play wi' it!'

'But . . . when you did know?'

'Man, then it was too late! You'd be thinkin' I was takin' ma cue from the chiel Collins. An' then I'd be in it up to ma neck, an' lettin' down Mr Frazer besides.'

Gently stared at him, shook his head. He said, 'So now perhaps we can have your true account. Why you went up Glen Eden on Monday, what you did there, and what you saw.'

'An' you'll no' be makin' a charge against me?'

'Only if you do not tell the truth.'

Scruffy Jock rasped his stubble. He stared at Gently once or twice. Outside a car passed in the street, and then again the night was silent. Scruffy Jock said:

'There's just nothin' to it! I was fancyin' a wee drive before ma lunch. And they'd been fixin' the timing on the car, so it wouldna be the worse for a bit o' a test run.'

'But why up Glen Eden?'

'Why? Because it's a sonsie spot, that's a'.'

'It wasn't because you knew you'd find Mrs Angus up there?'

'Ach, a' that was clean out o' ma heid! Na, I was fancyin' a wee drive awa' from the pumps an' the smell o' gasoline, an' where there wouldna be overmuch traffic, an' I might catch a glim o' a deer.'

Gently gave him a look. 'Go on.'

'Weel, I was sidlin' up the glen – just up to the loanin', you ken where – it's an awfu' rough road beyont there. An' I came on these two mannies, the doctor an' the puir young laddie. An' they was bawlin' awa' at each other like they was meanin' to come to blows.'

Gently said, 'Where were their cars parked?'

'Where? The doctor's was pu'd just off the road, an' the

young laddie's was driven on the strath – it's a' guid solid ground there.'

'And the two men – were they across by the broken-down willow?'

'Ach, no! They were one each side o' the laddie's car – it was a' that was keepin' them apart.'

'And Mrs Angus?'

'Na, she'd be hidin' out, I'm thinkin'.'

'You didn't see Mrs Angus at all?'

'Weel . . . I'm not just sayin' that.'

Gently stared hard. 'So carry on!'

Scruffy Jock flicked his hair. He said, 'I didna want to meddle wi' what was goin' on there, so I'm drivin' straight past an' roun' to the loanin', an' I'm hangin' on for a wee, still hearin' them bawlin' awa'. Then I'm hearin' a door slam, an' the doctor roarin', an' the sound o' a car racin' awa'. An' then a woman's voice . . . screamin'.'

Gently stared very hard. 'Go on.'

'Ach, I couldna ken whit was goin' to happen! She was oot there dingin' awa' at the doctor as I came past on my way down. Lettin' him have it, she was, an' he stood there takin' it, like he was struck out o' stone. An' I put ma foot down, an' left them to it. An' that's the last I saw o' them.'

'Fowler had gone.'

'Aye. He had.'

'Just Angus and his wife remained there.'

'Just themselves.'

'And you followed Fowler.'

Scruffy Jock nodded his greasy head.

'I see,' Gently said. He kept staring. 'Jock Mackay – isn't that what they call you?'

'Ach now, Scruffy Jock will do!'

Gently said, 'Mr Mackay, I wish to have a sight of your driving licence.'

'Ma . . . licence?'

'If you will.'

'But ma licence – it's a' in order!'

'Please produce it, Mr Mackay.'

Scruffy Jock sat rigid behind the table. Gently held out his

159

hand. Scruffy Jock sat staring at it with hooded eyes. Finally, and very slowly, he drew out a wallet, separated the licence and handed it to Gently. Gently opened it out. The name on the licence was: Stephen Wallace Jamieson. He looked back at Scruffy Jock. He found himself staring at the muzzle of an automatic pistol.

'I should warn you this is loaded,' Scruffy Jock said.

And the vernacular had stripped itself from his speech.

Another car passed slowly down the street, most probably one of the patrol cars. For an instant, Jamieson's eyes switched towards the sound, but returned immediately to Gently. Gently folded the licence again and laid it down on the table. He took his pipe from his pocket and began to fill it, his every movement watched by the other man. He said:

'I believe you had to leave Glasgow in a hurry.'

The muzzle of the automatic didn't waver.

'Something about a body taken from the Clyde. One person I've talked to thought it might have been yours.'

'Does that matter now?' Jamieson said.

'Probably not.' Gently struck a match. 'Just that, a little earlier, you were preparing to sue your ex-wife. Then you disappeared. And the body was recovered.' Gently lit his pipe. 'Possibly no connection?'

'That was ten years ago!'

'Who was that man?'

'Some human filth. It doesn't matter.'

'Perhaps an ex-associate in the drugs line?'

'If you know, why do you ask me?'

Gently puffed.

'All right, then,' Jamieson said. 'If it matters, that fellow was with me in Barlinnie. I met up with him again one night in a pub. He must have formed the impression that I was still in the business.'

'What happened?'

'He followed me out to the car-park. He stuck a knife in my ribs. He wanted a cut. I defended myself. Then I drove his body down to the river.'

160

'You removed the head?'

'With his own knife. He had been my cell-mate, I could have been connected. The head and hands I wrapped in newspaper and dumped later. In Lomond.'

'And left town.'

'Yes. That was the end, don't you understand?'

Gently puffed. Jamieson stared at him. The gun never ceased to point. Jamieson said:

'I'd lost everything – career, my marriage, my reputation. I'd been inside. And now I'd killed a man. That was the bottom. I had to get out.'

Gently said, 'So you killed yourself.'

'Yes. I suppose you could put it like that. The next day I swapped my car for this van, realized my few assets and hit the road north. Because myself I couldn't be any longer, what I'd been I had to get behind me. So I became a roadie, a Glasgow cop-out. I was at the bottom. I took it from there.'

'And . . . that brought you here.'

Jamieson tossed his hair irritably. 'I was down to my last fifty-pence piece. And the van was kaput. And so was I. Frazer offered me the job and I took it.'

'Did he never guess you weren't what you seemed?'

'He may have done. Perhaps he did.'

'And you stuck it – for another eight or nine years?'

'When you're at the bottom, you stay there.'

The lamp flickered. Jamieson glanced at it. Just briefly, the gun was lowered an inch. Gently put a fresh light to his pipe. Jamieson watched him. Gently said:

'Then, on Monday, your world touched you again.'

Jamieson nodded. 'Yes. Maureen.'

'You hadn't seen her since?'

'No. Maureen I'd put right out of my mind.'

'It must have been a shock.'

Jamieson looked away. He said, 'I didn't want to remember her. I kept my back turned while I was serving them, and tried to pretend to myself that I hadn't seen her. But it was no use. I knew I had to face her, and I knew just where I could find her.'

'Then . . . Angus arrived.'

161

'Yes. I cleared off and let Frazer deal with him. But that was what did it. I wanted to be there, to see the swine in the same situation as he had once put me in. I had Collins' car. I told Frazer I'd just give it a brief warm-up. That was usual, he didn't mind, and I took it away up the glen.'

'And the situation there was as you described?'

'They were facing each other across the car. Angus had his back to me. Fowler –' he tossed his hair – 'hadn't.'

Gently puffed, and stared. 'Go on.'

'I didn't see Maureen till I backed the car. Then I spotted her behind the bushes, watching what was going on. That was my chance. You won't believe me, but I had no intention of harming her. Just something drove me to face her out, to make her aware I was still alive. I got out of the car. I went over to her. I don't think she heard me till I was behind her. Then she turned, and saw who it was. And she opened her mouth to scream.'

'But she didn't succeed.'

The gun was drooping. 'I still can't believe it,' Jamieson said. 'I didn't mean it. I didn't want to hurt her. And then I was back in the car, driving away. Was it because I'd done the same thing before – can you be a killer without knowing you are one?'

Gently shook his head. 'And then there was Fowler.'

'Yes,' Jamieson said. 'Yes . . . Fowler.'

'He had recognized the driver of the car that passed.'

Jamieson said, 'I tried to talk to him.'

'You saw him by the phone-box.'

Jamieson nodded. 'He saw me too, and backed off towards the river. I went after him. It was the same. I only wanted to persuade him to keep his mouth shut. It was Angus you suspected, not him, and he had only to keep quiet.'

'He refused?'

'He got hysterical. He'd guessed what had happened in the glen. He began shouting and calling me a bloody murderer. I had to shut him up somehow.'

'Which', Gently said, 'brings us to this evening.'

Jamieson's stare fell to the gun. 'You . . . know?'

'Perhaps you'd better tell me.'

Jamieson jogged the gun in his hand. He said, 'He was here.'

'Angus was here?'

'Yes. He drove in here quite openly. I think he had decided to give himself up, but he wanted to be certain of something first.'

'When was this?'

'Around nine thirty. He pulled in and parked next to the van. If I'd seen him coming I'd have cleared off, but he didn't give me a chance.'

'What was he after?'

'He was asking me the precise time I dropped the car off for Collins, but then he stopped, and stared at me. No question about it he knew who I was.'

Gently said, 'Do you know where he is now?'

For a moment, Jamieson said nothing. Then, with his free hand, he felt in his pocket and took out a bunch of car keys. He threw them on the table.

'Angus's keys . . .?'

'Yes.'

'So where is he?'

'Look in the boot.'

'You – used that?'

'No, not this. I took it from the car. Angus always carried it.'

Slowly, Gently reached for the bunch of keys and laid them with the driving licence. He sat back. The gun still pointed. The night of the town continued silent. He said:

'What are your intentions now?'

Jamieson said tonelessly, 'Have I any option?'

'You can't walk away.'

'I've done it before.'

Gently said, 'This time is one too many.'

'I've got this,' Jamieson said.

'The police have many more.'

'I've got money. I took it from Angus.'

'Money isn't enough.'

'I know the country.'

Gently said, 'But do you know yourself?'

'You bastard,' Jamieson said.

'There's only one way back,' Gently said. 'For you, freedom

163

is no longer out there. It wasn't here, either. It's somewhere in yourself. You lost it when that body went into the Clyde.'

'I can still use this,' Jamieson said.

Gently shook his head. 'It can only use you.'

'I can tie you up, get away!'

'You would have to kill me.'

'Oh, you bastard!' Jamieson said.

Gently held out his hand. Jamieson stared at it. Sweat was glinting on his shadowed face. Of a sudden he snatched his face aside, and slammed the automatic on the table. It was a 9 mm. Browning. Gently picked it up and removed the magazine. The gun was fully loaded. He slipped shells and gun in his pocket. He said:

'When you're ready?'

Jamieson said nothing. Gently also picked up the licence and the keys. He rose to his feet. After a pause, Jamieson got to his feet likewise. Outside, he locked the door of the van. Gently held out his hand. Jamieson gave him the key. They walked across the yard and down the street to the police station, side by side, almost step for step. Only the duty man was present at the station; at Gently's instance, he put through a call to summon Blayne. Jamieson he sat down in the office. The duty man served them two mugs of sweet tea. Jamieson sat looking at his mug. He said:

'I'm mad. I have to be. Each time it was done before I knew what was happening. Maureen. The young man. And now Angus. The other one was just self-defence. Am I mad?'

Gently sipped tea.

'I meant to kill you too, you know that? As soon as I saw you I guessed you were on to me, and I nearly grabbed you right there at the door. Why didn't I kill you?'

'Drink your tea.'

'But why didn't it happen like the others?'

Gently said, 'Because it was over. And because Scruffy Jock was dead.'

'Because . . .?'

'The part you had played was over. You were having to become yourself again. It was no longer possible to prevent it, and killing again wouldn't have helped.'

164

'But you couldn't have known that!'

'It was a risk to take.'

'It could have been like the others.'

'Drink your tea.'

'I'm mad. It's the only possible answer.'

But Jamieson gulped some tea, and then sat silently staring at nothing. He still hadn't spoken another word when a car drew up, and Blayne, followed by Purdy, hastened into the office. Seeing the figure huddled on a chair, Blayne pulled up sharply.

'What's this then, you scruffy devil?'

Jamieson looked at him. He said, 'Perhaps you had better ask your friend here.'

'What – what?' Blayne's eyes were large. He stared at Jamieson, then at Gently. Gently said:

'This man is under arrest for the crimes recently committed here. On his own confession they also include the murder of Dr Angus.'

'But what are you sayin' – that Scruffy Jock – ?'

'Not Scruffy Jock!' Jamieson snarled.

'Ach, what am I hearin'!' Blayne exclaimed.

'Perhaps', Gently said, 'I should have a word with you?'

It was 2 a.m. by the time that Gently was at last able to leave the police station. By then the searchers had been recalled and the Mercedes recovered to reveal the gruesome contents of its boot. Angus, too, had been strangled, though not without putting up a struggle. An off-the-cuff examination of Jamieson revealed scratched wrists and fresh bruising under the stubble covering his jaw. The contents of his pockets included Angus's wallet, containing notes to the value of eight hundred pounds, and there were oily prints on the lid of the boot that would certainly link it with Angus's killer.

'Ach, it's game, set and match, man!'

Gently left it with the triumphant Blayne. He walked wearily up the street, past the garage, past the now-darkened van. The falls rushed under the bridge unobserved and there was no light at the mill, none at The Clachan. In the cottage he found

Gabrielle asleep on the settee, under a rug, with a cushion clutched to her.

'Oh, my dear! Where can you have been?'

'Hush!' Gently said. 'Don't wake the others.'

But Bridget's voice came sleepily from her bedroom:

'George, what sort of time do you call this?'

13

The excursion to Fort William went ahead largely because Bridget refused to let it die. The affair was regrettable but, after all, the transgressor had been arrested, and they had it on George's own authority that he had come quietly and given no trouble. It had perhaps meant a late night but George was used to those, and they had kindly allowed him to sleep late. So Bridget packed the picnic and filled the thermoses, and not long after ten they were shepherded to the cars.

'It's Saturday . . . there'll be quite a bit of traffic.'

Yes, but they were going against the tide in either direction: in the morning meeting the queues coming down from the north, in the evening those from the south scurrying to replace them. It perhaps took a little gloss off the expedition, but ensured that there should be few hold-ups.

And, after all, it proved a trip worth making, with a hazy sun to set off the great hills. At Tyndrum they turned north to run parallel with the railway and the engineering marvels that its route there insisted on. Followed Bridge of Orchy and the slanted climb up Black Mount, where, at the viewpoint, a kilted piper was skirling, then a slow descent into Rannoch Moor, with the snow-touched peaks of Glencoe ahead.

'And . . . it was over there?'

Yes: far, far off, across endless miles of bog, heather and bush, of lochans and scant willows, of tracks known only to the deer. The railway had left them at Loch Tulla to cross the wild to that preposterous station: the railway they would see no more until they met it again at Fort William.

'And today, he could have been alive . . .'

167

The miles seemed long across the moor, but at last they were diving and snaking down Glencoe among the giant peaks with their whitened brows. At Ballachulish a dainty suspension bridge had replaced the former ferry, and shortly they were cruising beside the sea loch, Loch Linnhe, and running into Fort William. They parked by the yacht-harbour and strolled in the town. Bridget bought cakes, and Gently tobacco.

'But . . . I wanted to see Ben Nevis!' Bridget complained. 'It's surely large enough. Why can't we see it?'

So they returned to the cars, and drove on, as far as the Commando Monument beyond Spean Bridge; and there had their picnic lunch with a mighty prospect of Nevis and its supporting hills. Also, at Spean Bridge, there was another attraction which Bridget could not bear to pass without sampling.

'That woollens warehouse . . .'

In the end, it beguiled each one of them into making a purchase: tweed jackets for the two men, a gorgeous knitted cardigan for Gabrielle, and for Bridget sufficient wool to keep her needles going till Christmas. So – a successful expedition! Yet, somehow, it wasn't quite that, either. There had been silences, thoughtful vacancies, a feeling of having escaped only on a lead. In the long twilight they drove back to Kinleary, past The Clachan, the falls, the mill. On their island the jackdaws seemed sombre, in the distance the ben looked sad.

'I'll cook those sausages . . .'

Geoffrey switched on the TV. And they caught the news at the wrong moment, just as a figure was being hustled from a police car: a figure that froze each one of them.

'I don't believe it – it isn't!'

A glimpse was all they caught of him, a glimpse of a man in a suit, clean-shaven, his short hair combed in a quiff.

'George, it just can't be him. You've made a mistake – they arrested someone else!'

But no: the commentator confirmed it: the prisoner was Stephen Wallace Jamieson, otherwise known as Jock Mackay.

'They've tidied him up, old girl. It's surprising what a little spadework can do.'

'But no, I could not recognize him either!' Gabrielle exclaimed. 'It is not the same man, surely?'

'George – what do you say?'

But Gently could only shake his head. Now they were being shown shots of the garage, of the van standing emptily in its corner of the yard. Jock Mackay was dead. He had died that moment when he had laid his driving licence on the table, when the gun had appeared in his hand, when the twang of the Gorbals had dropped from his speech. Stubble, greasy hair, stained jeans and all, the man he had arrested was Stephen Jamieson. What further point in a disguise? It was Jamieson who had committed the crimes.

'Well, they did a good job on him,' Geoffrey grinned. 'I'll bet even his boss doesn't know him now. He might even stand a chance – disrupted personality, something on those lines.'

'Geoffrey, you shouldn't jest about it,' Bridget said.

'There's always a case to make,' Geoffrey said. 'And when you think about it, none of this need have happened if they'd just rapped his knuckles over the drug business.'

'But', Gabrielle said, 'it did happen.'

'I'm going to cook the sausages,' Bridget said.

The news, meanwhile, had switched to politics and no longer held anyone's interest. Gabrielle looked at Gently, and sighed.

'I think I'll try on my new cardigan,' she said.

Brundall, 1992–93